"Put the gun down, Dr. Somers. We need to talk."

Zach had to believe that a doctor wouldn't take his life. She was in danger, and he couldn't walk away and live with himself—even if there was a long-running feud between their families.

"I have nothing to say to a Collier. Get off my land," Maggie demanded.

"You're in danger."

"You think?" She moved to the top of the steps, the shotgun still leveled at his chest.

"I'm not the cause of it. I came here to warn you."

She laughed, a humorless sound that filled the quiet. "Why do you think I would believe you?"

"Because your grandfather was murdered, just like mine."

Books by Margaret Daley

Love Inspired Suspense

Love Inspired

MARGARET DALEY

feels she has been blessed. She has been married more than thirty years to her husband, Mike, whom she met in college. He is a terrific support and her best friend. They have one son, Shaun. Margaret has been writing for many years and loves to tell a story. When she was a little girl, she would play with her dolls and make up stories about their lives. Now she writes these stories down. She especially enjoys weaving stories about families and how faith in God can sustain a person when things get tough. When she isn't writing, she is fortunate to be a teacher for students with special needs. Margaret has taught for over twenty years and loves working with her students. She has also been a Special Olympics coach and has participated in many sports with her students.

BURIED
SECRETS
Margaret
Daley

Steeple
Hill®

Published by Steeple Hill Books™

STEEPLE HILL BOOKS

Steeple
Hill®

ISBN-13: 978-0-373-44262-1
ISBN-10:   0-373-44262-9

BURIED SECRETS

www.SteepleHill.com

Printed in U.S.A.

But if from thence thou shalt seek
the Lord thy God, thou shalt find Him, if thou
seek Him with all thy heart and with all thy soul.
—*Deuteronomy* 4:29

To Laura, who enjoys adventures as I do

ONE

"Move and you're dead." Maggie Somers lifted the .22 higher, trying desperately to keep her hands from shaking. "I have a gun pointed at you."

The large man straightened, his back to her, rigid. "I had nothing to do with this." A piece of paper in his hand fluttered to the floor.

As her gaze swept the living room of her grandfather's ranch house, alarm snaked down her spine. *Everything's destroyed.* Tears stung her eyes, but she quickly blinked them back. There was no way this man was going to see any kind of weakness.

The intruder started to turn toward her.

"Don't move an inch." Her anger pushed aside her fear as she gripped the rifle tighter and placed her finger on the trigger.

"May I turn around and explain why I'm here?"

A steel thread weaved through his words, striking against her raw nerves. "Save your breath for the sheriff."

"Look, lady, this is ridiculous." Exasperation now edged his deep, husky voice.

Maggie stepped over the broken pieces of the Indian pottery that had sat on a table near the door, and moved farther into the room. The crunch beneath her shoes told her that more than the one priceless vessel from her grandfather's collection was shattered. Like alcohol in a festering wound, the sound toughened her resolve.

If only her cell worked out here on the ranch, she would have already called the sheriff and he'd be halfway here by now. She glanced at the phone across the room, then at the burglar—dressed in a black turtleneck and black jeans—and knew she had to do something with him before making the 9-1-1 call. If she let down her guard for a second, the man could easily overpower her.

"Pick up the extension cord near your feet. Slowly." She roughened her voice as much as possible, but to her own ears she sounded shaky.

The intruder remained still.

Her arm ached from holding the rifle to her shoulder. "Let me tell you something about myself. I'm an expert shot, and two of the things I hate in this world are liars and thieves. You're batting a hundred."

"Where do you want me?" His movements as he bent over and snatched up the cord conveyed his anger more than his words.

Anywhere but here. She searched her memory, trying to determine how this was done in the movies. "Sit in that rocking chair and tie your feet together."

He walked to it and stopped. "May I turn around now, or do you want me to sit in it backward?" Sarcasm sliced through his question.

"Slowly. Any sudden moves and I might get trigger-happy." She was sure she'd heard that in some cop movie.

"Will that make your day?"

He slowly faced her. His gaze locked with hers. The penetrating intensity in his stare unnerved her. As his slate-gray eyes—as cold as a tombstone—assessed her, she had the horrible thought that if he wanted, he could probably disarm her before she got a shot off. This man exuded danger. Why had she decided to come inside? Her heartbeat caught for a second, then battered against her chest. Why hadn't she run when she'd had the chance?

Because she had been so furious that someone had dared to defile her grandfather's memory on the day she had buried him that she hadn't been thinking straight.

She motioned with the rifle. "Sit."

The wooden rocking chair creaked as the intruder lowered himself into it. When he dropped his gaze from hers, she released a long sigh while he tied his ankles together with the cord Maggie had kicked to him.

Rugged features set in harsh lines greeted her perusal. Dark brown hair with touches of fire brushed his nape. His full lips and high cheekbones added to his commanding presence. Over six feet tall, lean and muscular, his frame reinforced that impression of lethal force.

"Does this meet with your approval?"

His insolent question drew her gaze back to his face. His voice held a steely quality that matched his look, as though he had stared down the barrel of a rifle before, and survived.

Fear tingled up her spine. She refused to answer him, but instead found another length of cord and walked a wide circle around the chair to stand behind it. Once he was tied up, she would be all right. "Give me your hands."

He complied. She quickly cradled the rifle between her legs, then looped the cord from the blinds around his wrists. The feel of his flesh against her fingers jolted her. For a long second she fumbled with the rope, almost dropping it. Sucking in a deep, fortifying breath, she hastened to finish the job, blocking from her mind the warmth of his skin against hers. Relief trembled through her as she grasped the .22 and backed away.

With her eyes cast downward, she knelt in front of him and checked the cord about his ankles. She felt the drill of his stare and fought the urge to quail. As she rose, her gaze finally trekked upward. The rage she saw in his expression took her breath away. This man wasn't accustomed to being subdued by anyone. She hurriedly moved toward the phone and picked it up.

"Do you seriously think I look like a thief? Would a thief drive a sports car like the one out front?" he asked after she made the call to the sheriff.

"You probably stole that, too."

"C'mon, lady. I did *not* have anything to do with this. I came here—"

"Oh," she said, cutting him off, "then you just make a habit of stopping by houses that have been ransacked to have a look around? Were you looking for some garage sale and made a wrong turn? Or perhaps you're an insurance adjuster getting a jump on the job?"

"No, I came to talk to you," he said through clenched teeth.

"Before or after you robbed me?" Her anger held her firmly now that he was tied up. She sat on the coffee table and laid the rifle across her lap. She settled one hand on her knee, the other on the .22, so she'd be prepared if the intruder tried anything.

"I came in after the fact. I did not rob you." Each word was spoken slowly, distinctly, as though he were talking to a child who didn't understand.

"That's what all the criminals say. I think you need to work on your delivery if you're going to get a jury to believe you." She raked her gaze down him, hoping to convey her contempt. "It lacks conviction."

He didn't say another word. His eyes said it all, boring into her with a ferocity that warned her never to be alone with this man.

As she waited for the sheriff, she drummed her fingers on her knee and tried to avoid looking at his eyes, and at the chaos about her. Which was very hard to do, especially the pottery that Gramps had found, each piece smashed beyond repair. She wasn't ready to deal with the mess. One crisis at a time. As a doctor, that was how she handled a medical emergency. That was how she would handle this, too.

Minutes stretched into fifteen, the tension-laden silence gnawing away at her fragile composure. The occasional times she caught the intruder's glare she felt as though she were a specimen under a microscope— pinned to the paper, unable to move, laid bare for examination. The feeling left her extremely uneasy.

"You're pretty isolated out here. It'll take the sheriff a while to ride to your rescue." His sarcasm broke the stillness.

"Is that why you picked this place? Its isolation?"

"I *picked* it because it's Jake Somers's ranch."

"You scum!" She shot to her feet, the .22 clutched in her hands. "You read about his funeral today and came here to rob the place while everyone was gone." She brought the weapon to her shoulder, chambering a bullet. She wanted this man to squirm for what he had done to her grandfather's memory, to his prized possessions, which he'd lovingly collected over the years.

Several heartbeats passed; Maggie stared into the man's cold eyes.

"It's true. I did read this morning about Jake's death and the funeral, but—"

"Shut up! Not another word."

Icy silence pervaded the room, heightening the strain even more.

Finally the sound of car doors slamming closed pulled her attention from the stranger. She lowered the rifle. The sheriff and one of his deputies entered the house and scanned the damage.

"Hello, Maggie. I see you've had some trouble." The sheriff pushed his hat up on his forehead.

"I'm so glad you're here, Tom. I caught this man going through my grandfather's things."

Tom's regard swung to the man in the rocking chair. "You did, did you? Is the whole house like this?" The sheriff gestured at the wreckage.

"I don't know. I haven't had a chance to check."

"Why don't you and Rob do a walk-through? Then he can take your statement while I take care of this stranger. We'll have him out of your hair in no time."

Glad to be out of the intruder's line of vision, Maggie led the way, with the deputy following. After checking the two bedrooms and finding everything in disarray, she headed for the kitchen, her grandfather's favorite room. When she saw the extent of the wreckage, she shuddered. Every drawer was dumped, each cabinet emptied, many dishes smashed. Food was scattered about, as boxes and containers had been ripped apart.

"Dr. Somers, can you tell if anything is missing?" While the deputy began inspecting the area, he withdrew his pad and pen from the front left pocket of his tan shirt.

Maggie pivoted, her gaze taking in the chaos about her, but her mind refusing to register the robbery's total impact. "I don't know. I probably won't know that for days, at the very least. Gramps didn't have a lot of valuable things, except for some Indian artifacts he'd collected. They were destroyed." She waved her hand toward the living room, remembering the shattered pottery underfoot. "This land was about it."

"Tell me what happened when you came to the ranch."

"When I pulled up, I saw the door wide-open and that sports car out front. I knew something was wrong. I know I shouldn't have come inside. But I was so angry. I got Gramps's .22 from his pickup and decided to see what was going on. All I wanted to do was catch the thief."

"You could have been hurt."

"I'd just buried my grandfather and someone was trying to steal his things. I wasn't going to let that happen. Besides, Gramps taught me how to shoot, to take care of myself."

"You said you found that man going through your grandfather's belongings. Is that right?"

Remembering back to the first few seconds when she had seen the intruder in the living room made her breath come up short. She took several deep inhalations to fill her oxygen-deprived lungs. "When I came into the house, he was standing by a table, looking at the contents of a drawer piled on top of it. He held a piece of paper, which he dropped when he heard me."

"We'll take him to the station and sort through this mess. I'll give you a few days to see what's missing. You'll need to file it with us for insurance purposes, but I suspect there's nothing missing, since you interrupted the man."

"Probably not, but the damage has been done." She waved her arm at the disarray.

Maggie trailed after the deputy into the living room. The sheriff had the intruder handcuffed and was reading him his rights. She took great pleasure in watching the scene. She hoped they threw the book at the thief for trying to rob a dead man.

When Tom asked the stranger if he understood his rights, the man looked straight at her. "Yes, I understand perfectly."

"Where are your keys?" the sheriff asked the man.

"In my front right pocket."

"My deputy will follow us to the station in your car," Tom said, retrieving the keys from the trespasser, "and we'll check out your story."

The intruder's stare knifed through Maggie like an Arctic gale. Shivering, she spun away as the officers led the thief outside.

When the cars left, Maggie picked up the rifle and walked outside. She placed the .22 on the gun rack in her grandfather's black truck, near the barn where she had parked her Mustang so that whoever was in the house wouldn't hear her arrival. Yes, she'd known how to shoot since she was a young girl, but as a doctor she'd seen what people could do with a gun and she hadn't picked one up in years.

After slamming the truck door shut and locking it, she stood and let the silence enfold her in its comforting embrace. For days people had surrounded her, giving her no time to think, to feel.

Now she was finally alone.

She leaned against the pickup and stared at a mesa in the distance. Stark, sharp lines jutted upward toward the sky. Sunlight glittered off the red-and-white surfaces of the rock. In this land of harsh beauty, the mesa stood alone, like her. Suddenly, with all that had happened in the past hour, she couldn't handle the solitude she had sought so desperately after the funeral. The quiet screamed at her, declaring to the world just how defenseless she was, miles from Santa Fe, alone, with only the wind's whisper and the occasional rustle of an animal scurrying across the yard.

She peered at the dirt road leading to the highway,

at the remains of the dust kicked up by the cars settling back into place, as if nothing had happened. Alone, until someone intruded, she thought. Why? What did Gramps have that the creep would want?

Most likely nothing was gone. Anything the intruder had taken would have been on his person or in his car, and the sheriff would recover that. Unless someone else had been with him and had already left. The scope of the destruction was vast, almost too much for one man. She would never know if something was missing unless she went inside and started the laborious task of straightening up.

Shoving away from the truck, she scanned the ranch. *Mine now.* The feelings she'd held at bay for three days inundated her all at once. Anger, bereavement and a bone-weary tiredness flooded her and made her steps leaden as she trudged toward the house.

On the porch she paused, not wanting to go back to the chaotic mess in the house that had once been so neat and orderly. She whirled around and stared off into the distance, at the top of the mesa near the highway. She watched a lone hawk circle, looking for its prey. Then suddenly the bird swooped down for the kill. Maggie closed her eyes. She couldn't take seeing the hawk rise triumphantly with its catch in its talons. That man today had made her feel like helpless prey, vulnerable, afraid and not in control. She'd struggled never to feel those emotions again.

"What am I going to do, Gramps?" she whispered, needing to hear the sound of her own voice. With his death, she had no family left. She was as alone as that bird's quarry. As alone as that time... No, she wouldn't think about the past.

A dull throb began to pound behind her eyes. She massaged her temples, putting off for a few more seconds what she knew must be done.

When she went inside, the raw impact of the destruction hit her all over again. Everything she loved and cared about was strewn and ripped apart before her. Drawers were emptied, their contents flung all around. The cushions on the chairs and couch were sliced open to reveal the stuffing. Cherished photos were tossed on the floor, the glass from the frames shattered.

In the midst of the disarray, pages of the old family Bible, torn and crumpled, lay scattered about the room. She might be angry with the Lord for taking yet another loved one, but the sight ripped through what composure she had left. What kind of monster could do that to the Bible?

A picture of the intruder invaded her thoughts and iced her blood. Tears pooled in her eyes and streaked down her cheeks. Her grandfather's possessions were her last link to him. All destroyed! Bewildered, she took a few more steps into the middle of the living room. Slowly she turned in a full circle, feeling as though she were in a dream, none of this real.

But it was very real.

She bent down and found the Bible partially hidden beneath the couch. She sank down onto the coffee table and fingered the black leather of the book, which was missing most of its pages. Her grandfather had treasured this above all, and it was beyond repair. It had been in

her family for almost a hundred years. Through the
sheen of tears she tried to gather the crushed pages into
a pile. Her vision blurred, she blinked several times. The
tears flowed even more. She gave up and allowed them
to fall.

Finally, when she had no tears left to shed, she wiped
her cheeks with the back of her hand and started once
again to pick up the pages of Gramps's beloved Bible.
Once she had collected all of them, she moved to the
contents of the drawer covering part of the coffee table
and tried to bring some kind of order to it. Then she
went to another disheveled pile and did the same.

Evening shadows crept into the room, forcing Maggie to switch on a light. Still she labored, determined
to make the living room look like it had when she had
left for the funeral that morning. No one was going to
come into her life and totally disrupt it as that man had
earlier. She'd had too much of that in the past. She
wasn't going to allow it. She'd finally managed to have
some control over her life, and she wasn't going to give
it up without a fight.

After hours of working nonstop, Maggie rose and
stretched her cramped, aching muscles. The pounding
in her head had subsided to a dull throb, but her eyes
felt heavy, gritty. She glanced at the mess still about her.
It wasn't going anywhere, and she needed coffee.

In the kitchen, she waited at the sink for the brew to
percolate, staring out the window at the darkness. The
feeling of total isolation swamped her again, suddenly
making her quake in the warm night air. The lock on the
front door was flimsy, obviously not a good deterrent. She

should leave and return some other day with several friends to help her, to keep her company, she thought to herself.

She would only stay a little longer.

The scent of coffee infused the night, temporarily reviving her spent body. Reviving her soul was a lost cause.

She poured herself a cup, took a few sips and started for the living room. She would finish the cabinet and then call it quits. As she reentered, the phone's jarring ring startled her, and she nearly dropped her mug.

Hurrying to answer the call, she picked up the receiver. "Hello?"

"Maggie, this is Tom. Just wanted to tell you we let the man go."

Her grip tightened. "Why?"

"Because his story checked out. He's a respected professor at Albuquerque City College. He had an alibi for most of the day, except the time it would have taken him to drive to the ranch. There's no way he could have been there long enough to do the kind of damage I saw."

"Who is he?"

"Dr. Zach Collier."

The man's name renewed her seething emotions. "I want him arrested for trespassing, then."

"Now, Maggie, I know you're upset about what happened, but the man only came inside because he thought you were there and in danger."

"A Collier would never feel that way about a Somers. He's lying." Ever since she could remember, she had heard that from her grandfather, and after what Red Collier had done to Gramps, she believed him.

"Sleep on it. If you still feel that way tomorrow, come see me. Go home, Maggie."

After hanging up, she lifted her mug to her lips and drank. The brew flowed down her throat, warming her cold insides. The sheriff might believe Zach Collier didn't have anything to do with this destruction, but she didn't. Somehow he was behind it. First thing tomorrow morning, she would be at the sheriff station, demanding Tom file trespassing charges against the man.

The sound of a car approaching the house diverted her attention toward the front door. For a second she thought of calling the sheriff back, but it would take twenty minutes for him to get to the ranch. Besides, it could be any number of Gramps's friends.

Maggie hurried across the room. Flipping on an outside light, she stepped out onto the porch and saw a red sports car come to a stop. She flew back inside and rushed to the mantel, where Gramps kept his shotgun. With no time to call the sheriff, she grabbed it as she heard a car door slam closed.

Back out on the porch, she lifted the shotgun and said, "Come any closer and I'll shoot you."

TWO

Zach unfolded his long body from his Corvette and stood, wondering why in the world he was back out at Jake Somers's ranch. *Fool.* He'd called himself that several times as he'd driven to the scene of his earlier humiliation. And now, seeing Maggie Somers pointing a shotgun at him, he berated himself for not listening to that little voice inside him.

But she was in danger, and he couldn't walk away and live with himself. *Father, protect me and help me make her see the truth.*

"Put the gun down. We need to talk." He schooled his voice in a calm cadence, hoping to soothe her. He had to believe that a doctor wouldn't take his life, even if there was a long-running feud between their families.

"I have nothing to say to a Collier. Get off my land."

"You're in danger."

"You think?" She moved to the top of the steps, the shotgun still leveled at his chest.

"And I'm not the cause of it. I came here to warn you."

She laughed, a humorless sound that filled the quiet.

"Do I have *stupid* written on my forehead? Why do you think I would believe you?"

"Because your grandfather was murdered."

"Murdered?" Maggie stiffened, the shotgun wavering, dropping slightly from her shoulder. "My grandfather died in a riding accident. The sheriff didn't find any foul play."

"I believe it was murder because my grandfather died under similar circumstances recently."

She again secured the weapon firmly at her shoulder. "I've listened. Consider me warned. You've done your good deed for the day. Now, leave."

Father, give me the right words to say to this woman. "I'm not my grandfather. The feud was between them, not us."

"You're a Collier. That's all I need to know."

"Three weeks ago my grandfather died in a rehabilitation center. His death didn't raise any questions because he had a stroke. But his room at the center was searched. At first I didn't think too much about it, thinking an employee had been rummaging through his things. Then, while I was at the funeral, someone ransacked his house, too, and stole something of great value to my grandfather. Now I'm not so sure he died from natural causes, but he was cremated, so an autopsy can't be performed. I don't like coincidences. This is too similar to what happened at my granddad's house."

The throbbing in Maggie's head returned with an intensity that left her reeling. She needed twenty-four hours of sleep. She needed to be alone, safe. She needed to be in control. "There's no connection between your grandfather and mine. Yours took care of that almost sixty years ago." Exhaustion clung to her like a second skin. Arms aching, she lowered the shotgun but kept a tight grip on it.

"The diary is the connection."

His words brought her up straight. "Father Santiago's diary? But my grandfather could never find anything. He had decided it was a legend after all."

"He only had half the information."

Fury chased away her weariness. "Only because your grandfather stole the map from him. Do you know why my grandfather kept the diary instead of donating it to a museum? It reminded him of a man's potential for evil—one particular man's potential."

Zach Collier took several steps closer, charging the air with his power. "There's always two sides to an issue."

"Issue! A man's betrayal isn't an issue. Leave now, Dr. Collier." Contempt laced her voice.

"Think about what I said. You're in danger, especially if the person who did this didn't find the diary. When you come to your senses, you can reach me at Albuquerque City College. I have an office there in the science building. But don't wait too long. I'm leaving soon on an expedition."

Maggie didn't say anything as he left, the tension in the air evaporating as quickly as water in the desert. Her legs weak, her pulse pounding, she sank down on the top step. As she struggled to bring some kind of order to her thoughts, she scanned the terrain, inky darkness surrounding her. She couldn't stay another moment. She had to leave.

She quickly reentered the house, turned off the lights and locked up—not that it had done much good earlier. Stepping out onto the porch again, she inhaled deeply, the fresh air calming her frayed emotions. The man's theory of murder unnerved her more than the break-in. Zach Collier had obviously set out to frighten her, and for a little while she had allowed him to. Well, not anymore. She headed for her white Mustang.

She inserted a classical CD into the slot and turned up the volume. The music of Tchaikovsky filled the car. She emptied her mind of all but the music and the road stretching ahead of her.

Until she reached the outskirts of Santa Fe, Maggie didn't think much about the car behind her on the highway. But in town, every turn she made, the vehicle behind her did, too. She switched off the CD player and sat up, alert, tense. She was being followed.

Who was it? Collier?

She pressed her foot down on the accelerator. The car behind her increased its speed, too. In the dark she tried to see if it was Zach Collier in his red sports car, but all she saw were the headlights glaring brightly, obliterating her view. She wouldn't put it past that man to try to intimidate her further. Her grip on the steering wheel tightened as she thought of him behind her, intentionally trying to frighten her.

Maggie neared an intersection and at the last second swerved across two lanes of traffic to turn down a side street. When she chanced a glance in the rearview mirror, she noticed the car following her had copied her actions.

Sweat beaded on her forehead. *I can't go home. I won't lead whoever is behind me to my house. I need people.*

An idea took root in her mind. She headed for the hospital she worked at. Parking at the emergency entrance, she hopped out of her Mustang and ran into the building, glancing over her shoulder. She glimpsed several cars coming into the parking lot—none red Corvettes.

"Al, will you be a dear and park my car in the doctors' parking lot?" she asked an orderly when she saw him in the hall.

"Sure, Dr. Somers."

"Thanks." She flipped her keys to him as she hurried down the hallway, the swish of the automatic doors to the emergency room sounding as they opened. "Just put the keys in my mailbox when you've got a chance."

She again looked back, but all she saw were a mother and her son coming into the hospital. Was the person still outside waiting for her to leave? Was it Zach Collier? Had she imagined being followed?

The bustle of people comforted her as she made her way to a doctors' lounge on the second floor. She crossed to the window overlooking the main parking lot, to inch open the blind's slats. She searched the rows of vehicles. Still no red sports car. But there were other places for someone to sit and wait for her to emerge from the hospital, especially now that the person had been alerted to the fact that Maggie knew she was being followed.

She snatched up the phone and ordered a cab to pick her up at the service entrance in fifteen minutes. Pacing the room, she kept glancing at the window as though that would produce the car that had been behind her since she left the ranch. She hoped that if it was Zach Collier he would sit in his Corvette for hours waiting for her to come back outside. Too bad it wasn't freezing. And if it wasn't him— She wouldn't think about that. It had to be him. He had to be wrong about her grandfather being murdered.

Ten minutes later, she eased open the door to the doctors' lounge and checked the hallway. Two nurses stood at a counter at the end, and the elevator opened to reveal an older couple getting off. She hurried toward the elevator and slipped inside, punching the button for the basement level, where the service entrance was. Her heart hammered a maddening beat. She took several deep breaths to slow its pace.

She was letting a Collier's fantastical ravings get her all worked up. *Lord, why are You doing this to me? Wasn't it enough You took Gramps?*

When the elevator reached the lower floor, Maggie peered up and down the hallway. Empty. Where was everyone? Home, where she should be. She realized most of the labs and offices were on this level and that the majority of the people were gone by now.

She stepped out, and the doors swished closed. The click of her heels echoed down the long corridor as she walked toward the exit. The hairs on her nape tingled. She quickened her pace and peered back several times. Nothing. Yet.

Reaching the service door, she pushed it open and surveyed the area. Again, nothing. Lights from a car swept through the darkness and blended with the security lights. She squinted and made out the lines of a cab. It came to a stop ten feet away. She rushed toward it.

Slipping inside, she gave the driver her address, then slid down in the backseat so she wasn't visible to someone on the street. Several blocks away from the hospital, she inched up and glanced around. The empty street calmed the frantic beating of her heart, and she inhaled enough air to fill her lungs.

Leaning back against the cushion, she closed her eyes, and immediately the image of Zach Collier materialized in her thoughts. She shivered. Never in her life had she had a day like this one. She tried to get a handle on all that had happened, but her exhausted mind refused to think beyond one thought: she could be in danger.

When the taxi pulled up outside her house, she scanned the street, searching for anything unfamiliar. She felt as though she were in the middle of a spy story, caught up in the intrigue. She paid the driver, then walked quickly toward her front door. After fumbling around in her purse, she withdrew her key and inserted it into the lock.

A dog barked next door.

She jumped, her purse slipping from her grasp. Her nerves raw, she snatched up the large leather bag and threw a quick look over her shoulder, as if she expected someone to rush up the sidewalk or leap out from the bushes by the porch.

A sigh trembled past her lips. Empty. She hurriedly

entered her house, immediately flipping on a light. The bright glow killed the darkness, and she sank back against the closed front door, her body quaking. When she peered into the living room off to the right, half expecting to see a chaotic mess, she slid to the tile floor. Relief mingling with exhaustion swept through her. Everything was in perfect order, as neat and tidy as always.

She should get some rest—put this whole day behind her—but the blur of the past few hours numbed her. She clasped her legs and lay her head on her knees. This time she didn't close her eyes, and yet she pictured Zach Collier as though he stood in her entryway, as arrogant and audacious as earlier.

What if he was right, and someone had killed Gramps? What if he hadn't been the person behind her on the highway? What if Gramps's killer had been tailing her into town, watching her at the ranch? Maggie sat up straight. She realized in that moment that she wouldn't be able to rest until she knew the truth about his death. And the place to start was the diary.

She shoved to her feet and headed for her bedroom, the first room she'd put in order when she'd moved in a few weeks ago. She spent most of her time in it. When she entered, she bypassed her king-sized, four-poster bed and headed for the armoire. She opened the bottom drawer. An old black book, protected in a temperature- and humidity-controlled case, lay nestled among her sweaters. Her hands quivered as she carefully lifted it out.

Had Gramps died for this?

She opened the case. Cautiously, because the aged pages were fragile, she perused the diary, written by a Spanish monk during the sixteenth century. His handwriting was bold and daring. She'd often thought the man must have been like his handwriting, if what he had written about his journey was true. Had he really found evidence of a lost group of Aztecs who had settled in the southwestern part of the United States? Had they carried with them some of the codices that experts thought had been destroyed by the Spanish conquerors? Could the diary and map really lead to where the codices were hidden? Or was it all a legend, as Gramps had come to believe in the end?

She settled onto her bed, carefully laying the diary, still in its case, in her lap. Her grandfather had given it to her on her thirtieth birthday, two years before, because she had always loved hearing about it. The diary had been one of his most prized possessions, yet he had parted with it because of his love for Maggie. If he had been murdered, she had to find the person responsible and make sure he paid for it. And if that meant working with Zach Collier, then she would—just as soon as she checked out his story about his grandfather's death.

THREE

Maggie stared at the Indian pottery—from various nearby pueblos in a cabinet in the lobby of the science building at Albuquerque City College. The brown, white and black geometric lines blurred as her thoughts became a tangle of possibilities. The receptionist had told her Dr. Zach Collier wasn't expected on campus because he didn't have any classes that day, which seemed strange in light of what he had told her the night before.

The young woman must have surmised that the disappointment in Maggie's expression was due to the fact she wouldn't get to bask in the man's presence. Shortly afterward, the receptionist had begun telling Maggie how popular Dr. Collier was with the students. His classes were in demand and filled within one hour of registration.

She should have called ahead to see if he would be here, but she hadn't wanted to alert him to her coming. What a waste! She'd even arranged for another doctor to take her patients this afternoon.

After loitering in the lobby for thirty minutes and

still undecided as to what to do, Maggie returned to the reeptionist's desk to see if she could persuade the woman to give her Dr. Collier's home phone number. Five minutes into all the reasons Maggie needed to get hold of him, a dreamy look appeared on the woman's face, and Maggie wondered if the young lady would swoon in her chair from just talking about the man.

A tingle pricked Maggie's nape. She rotated slowly and found Zach Collier striding toward her. His body conveyed a leashed energy ready at a second's notice to explode into action. The man before her had a manner and confidence about him that couldn't be feigned.

He paused at the desk. "Good afternoon, Kim."

The receptionist smiled. "I was just telling this woman you wouldn't be in today."

"A change in plans. We'll be in my office, but I'd prefer my presence here be kept a secret."

Surprise flitted across Kim's face as her gaze swung from Dr. Collier to Maggie. "Sure."

Zach indicated for Maggie to go first toward a hallway behind the receptionist's desk. "My office is the third one on the right."

Maggie made her way to the door and stopped. Okay, so everyone at the college thought the world of Dr. Zach Collier. That didn't mean he wasn't behind whatever was going on—and she still wasn't sure what that was. She needed to be cautious. After years of conditioning by Gramps, she wouldn't easily trust anyone with the last name Collier, no matter how persuasive he could be or how popular he was with his students and the college staff.

He unlocked his door and waved her inside. "I must say I wasn't expecting a change of heart this fast, but I'm glad you want to work with me."

Maggie froze a few feet into the office, then pivoted toward the man. "Work with you? I never said I was going to do that." The very idea still didn't sit well with her, even though logically she knew she should work with him if she wanted to find out what was going on.

"Then why are you here?"

The sound of the door clicking closed shimmied down her. "You know, that is a good question."

He arched a brow. "And? Are you going to answer it?"

"No." Because she didn't have an answer. Why was she here? In the light of a new day she wondered if what had happened less than twenty-four hours ago was all a dream. The one thing she did know was that her grandfather would be furious if he knew she was talking with the enemy.

"So you aren't convinced that Jake Somers was murdered?"

"Gramps's horse got spooked, and it threw him. That wasn't the first time he had fallen from one. This time he hit his head on a rock." As she stated the facts told to her by the sheriff, she tried to distance herself from the situation, but she couldn't shake the vision of Gramps lying at the top of the mesa for half a day until his body had been discovered by a ranch hand, who had found her grandfather's horse riderless near the barn.

"Accidents can be faked. How do you explain your grandfather's house being ransacked yesterday, like my grandfather's was?"

"Everyone knew about Gramps's funeral." Of course, those people were his friends and neighbors, whom she couldn't imagine robbing him. So the possibility that Zach Collier might be right had taken root in her mind while she had tossed and turned in her bed. Finally at five in the morning she'd given up the pretense of sleeping, and had done some research concerning Zach Collier on the Internet. She'd read about his grandfather's death and about Zach's disappearance the year before in the Amazon. Everyone had thought he was dead until his sister, Kate, had found him living with a tribe of Indians in a remote part of the jungle.

Zach went behind his desk and sat. "Was anything taken?"

"I don't know. I still have a lot to clean up." She lowered herself onto a chair nearby, and although a desk separated them, the room was too small, too intimate with its wall-to-wall bookcases filled with Indian artifacts interspersed among scientific volumes, mostly dealing with chemistry and biology. She felt enclosed in a tomb, drawn toward this man against her better judgment.

"I noticed the television was still there. His guns. Those are items a robber would steal."

"True." And Gramps's prized Indian collection had been trashed, not stolen. "Maybe you scared them away." She was grasping at straws, but she just wasn't ready to admit to the possibility her grandfather had been murdered. The implication shook her very foundation.

"So you don't think my theory holds up?" He tapped his fingers against the padded arm of his chair.

"I didn't say that. I'm here to listen. I owe that much to Gramps."

He glanced at his watch. "It's nearly dinnertime. Let's go someplace and eat. I talk better on a full stomach."

"So like a man to say that," she muttered as she rose.

He chuckled. "So much of my life has been spent in primitive surroundings searching for the next wonder drug, that when I can I indulge in the finer things in life, like good food."

"I read in the newspaper last year about your company's troubles."

His eyes widened. "You read about a Collier?"

"I like to be informed about the family enemy. Actually, Gramps took great pleasure in showing me the article. You lost the company?"

He shrugged. "One of my partners was dealing in illegal drugs. By the time the dust settled the company was in shambles."

"So you came here?" Maggie gestured around her.

"My grandfather needed me. I came to be close to him and do something different with my life. I've discovered I enjoy teaching, as well as researching. Here I get to do both."

When Maggie walked to the office door, Zach reached around to open it. His arm grazed hers. An electrical jolt streaked through her. It took all her willpower not to jump back from his touch, not to show him that he could make her react to his very nearness. She sent him a shaky smile as she stepped into the corridor. He returned it with a mind-shattering one that made her legs wobble.

While she strode next to him toward the parking lot, she tried to steel herself against the charm that seemed to come to him so effortlessly today. She reminded herself that he wanted something from her, so of course he would turn it on. It could probably be turned off just as easily. She recalled the evening before. Right now he fit into the civilized environment around him, but she strongly suspected he was more at home in the jungle, with its raw primitiveness. The article she had read had recounted the story of him being lost in the Amazon for weeks, and his near death. His life had been saved by a group of Indians who shunned outsiders, and yet had taken him into their tribe.

"You can follow me, or I can drive and bring you back later. I have to come back anyway to do some work tonight." Zach paused at her car.

"Your hours are as bad as a medical doctor's."

"At the end of the term, I'm mounting an expedition into the jungle, so there's work to be done. I do it when I can. I have four weeks to get everything done."

"And find your grandfather's killer, too?"

His look sharpened. "And yours. I'll make the time if I have to. I owe my grandfather a lot."

As she did hers. The thought emphasized a bond between them she wished she could deny. They each loved their grandfathers. "I'll ride with you. It'll give us more time to talk."

Zach indicated his red sports car a few spaces away. "Bought and paid for by *me*."

Heat singed her cheeks.

"Another one of my indulgences," he explained. "I

love to feel power beneath me, and I have a fondness for old cars."

"I guess it beats riding donkeys or walking." She followed him to his classic 1968 Corvette.

"Don't get me wrong. I like the jungle. There's something about it that keeps drawing me back."

That fit him. Zach Collier had a way of stripping away civilization to its primeval core. His lean power, leashed at the moment, made her wary. He was a dangerous man on more than one level, different from anyone she had met. She knew his partner had tried to kill him, and he had survived.

Seated in his car, Maggie let the silence linger between them as he weaved his way through traffic. She didn't look at him, but instead concentrated on the view to her side. Although she'd said they could talk on the way to the restaurant, she was tired, plain and simple. That was the only reason this man was getting to her. After spending part of the morning researching him on the Internet, she was beginning to wonder if there was anything he couldn't do. He had several doctorates and knew many languages. His interests were varied—from finding a new drug in the wilds of the rain forest to spending time with an isolated tribe of Indians. He had come into her grandfather's house yesterday, stared down the barrel of a rifle and not flinched.

She leaned back, letting the smooth ride lure her into a semiconscious state. If she could just catch up on her sleep, she was sure she would be her old self again—confident, in control, her thoughts neat and organized, not centered on the man next to her.

When Zach pulled into a parking lot at a Mexican restaurant in the foothills of Albuquerque, she didn't want to get out. That meant she would have to listen to him tell her why he thought her grandfather had been murdered. Suddenly the thought of someone deliberately causing Gramps's riding accident knotted her stomach. It also meant, if Zach was right, that she was in danger from some unknown source because she had the diary, and she suspected that someone knew it. Was that the person who'd followed her last night? In the back of her mind, she'd hoped it had been Zach.

"After you left last night, what did you do?" She climbed from the Corvette.

The mention of the evening before caused his eyes to become diamond hard. "Went home to nurse my wounded pride. I never thought I would have such a difficult time convincing someone she may be in danger. Of course, I've never been arrested before, either."

Maggie paused at the entrance into the restaurant. "You didn't follow me into Santa Fe?" She was ninety percent sure of the answer, but she needed to hear it from him.

"No, I live here." When she started to open the door, he placed a hand on her arm and swung her around to face him. "Why? Did something happen after I left?"

The feel of his fingers on her momentarily captivated her attention.

"Maggie, what happened?"

"I was followed into town."

"That must mean the person doesn't have the diary, then."

"It's not at my grandfather's house." She couldn't tell

him everything just yet. She couldn't shake off the years of hating the name Collier overnight. She wasn't even sure if it would ever be possible to completely trust someone with that last name, however irrational that might sound. By his own admission Zach had been close to Red Collier, and that man would have given anything to have the map *and* the diary, had tried years ago to be the sole owner of both. Was Zach fulfilling a deathbed wish to get the monk's journal and solve the mystery of the lost Aztecs and their codices? Her thoughts chilled her. She normally wasn't a person who mistrusted and questioned every move someone made, but after the day before, she would be doing that more. Her life might very well depend on it.

"If they have the diary, then why follow you?" Zach asked after they had been seated and the waitress had taken their orders.

"That's the first question we can ask them when we find them." She hoped her flippant answer would keep him from probing any deeper, because she couldn't out-and-out lie to him. She'd never been a good actress.

He rubbed the back of his neck, his forehead furrowed. "This whole business doesn't make a whole lot of sense. Our grandfathers have had the map and diary for years. Why the interest in them now?"

"Exactly. I'm still not totally convinced anything is going on."

"What will it take to convince you?"

"You say you weren't the one who followed me, but—"

He bent forward, his eyes pinpoints, anger slashing his face. "Do you have to get killed to believe me? Something is going on, and the person behind it won't stop until he gets what he wants. As to why now, I'm not sure. It wasn't common knowledge that our grandfathers had the map and diary. Maybe one of them talked."

"In recent years Gramps had decided the rumors he had heard years ago were just that, rumors based on legend, not facts. He didn't think the diary was important to anyone but him. He retrieved all the information he needed for his anthropological study of the Aztec Indians at the time of the Spanish conquest, but he never discussed the diary with anyone but me and my father. I don't even think my mother knew about it." She folded her arms and glared across the table at him. "Gramps didn't say anything."

Zach averted his gaze for a few seconds. "I can't say that about my granddad. He had a stroke a couple of months ago, and he would sometimes ramble on about the past. He could have said something. But most people probably wouldn't have realized what he was talking about."

"But maybe one did?"

He nodded.

"Do you know who visited him?"

"Not for sure. A lot of his old colleagues from the college came to see him, but the rehabilitation center didn't keep a list of visitors. I asked."

She was well aware that Red Collier had gone on to garner quite a reputation in the field of archaeology, and had taught at the same college as Zach. "Too bad. We could have started with that."

"We can try interviewing members of the staff and see if anyone remembers anything."

"That might be a good idea."

"Whoever is after this legend won't be giving it to any museum. It has to be a private collector." Anger cut deep into his features. "I can't tolerate knowledge lost for private gains."

She thought of what her grandfather had hoped to glean from the information written on the deerskins about the lost sect of Aztecs, if indeed, they had fled to the Southwest ahead of the Spanish conquerors. "I know one of your areas of expertise is anthropology, like my grandfather. It could sure enhance your reputation if you discovered the codices and evidence of the lost Aztec tribe who tried to preserve part of their culture from the Spanish conquistadors."

The harsh glint in Zach's eyes stabbed her. "The reason you can say that, Dr. Somers, is because you don't know me at all. Was that comment made because I'm a Collier? Do you judge a man without getting to know him?" The taut lines of his body transmitted his feelings more than his quiet words, spoken with a lethal edge.

Her gaze fixed upon the nerve that twitched in the hardened line of his jaw, and she regretted her words. She moistened her dry lips. "No, not usually."

"The most important reason I want to find the codices is that it was Granddad's lifelong dream. He believed they existed to the day he died. He wanted to prove once and for all a group of Aztecs had lived in the Southwest, separated from the ones near Mexico City. He believed the legend that they had taken some of the Aztec treasures with them for safekeeping." He brought his glass of water to his lips, his gaze never leaving hers. "It may have been wishful thinking on my grandfather's part, because he hated to admit that something of such historical significance would have been destroyed by the Spanish."

The intense way he was looking at her made her realize how lacking she was in the ways of men and women. Except for her one relationship in college with Brad Wentworth, she hadn't dated much, having devoted her life to her studies and becoming a doctor. Now that she was established in a thriving practice, she still didn't date much.

She breathed in sharply and caught the scent of him, enticingly masculine—clean, fresh, like the desert at night. When his regard dropped to the pulse beat at her throat, his look entranced her. Then slowly his gaze reconnected with hers, and the earlier bond she had experienced grew.

For a long moment she couldn't think clearly. Then, from a willpower she was beginning to realize was lacking more and more around him, she glanced away. She had to focus on what was important: the map and diary that could lead to the Aztec codices. "Was the map stolen?" she asked finally.

"Yes."

The anxiety in the air between them settled around her shoulders heavily, weighing her down as though it were an iron cloak. "Then what's the use? If the legend is right, you have to have both the map and the diary to find the location of the codices and any other Aztec treasure there may be."

He straightened, alert. "Because I have a copy of the map. Do you have a copy of the diary?"

"No, and even if I did, why should I trust you?" Red Collier had betrayed Gramps; taking the map and his true love, Willow-in-the-Wind, for his wife. If the man had been able to steal the journal from her grandfather, he would have done that, too. She had grown up knowing every minute detail of the feud between the two men, which had started over a woman they'd both loved and a treasure they had both wanted to find, first as partners, later as enemies.

"Because I don't want you to end up like your grandfather—dead."

His directness sizzled the air. Did he know she had the diary?

Thankfully, the waitress arrived with their dinners, and the moment shattered like a rock hitting a window. Maggie picked up her fork and started to eat. "I worked through lunch, fitting some afternoon patients in so I could come see you. I didn't eat anything. I'm starved, and this looks delicious."

"I see you're still not totally convinced someone killed your grandfather."

"No. As you said earlier, it's just a theory. No real proof."

"A scientist to the end. I can appreciate that. I hope, however, that that end isn't a permanent one."

She tightened her hold on her fork. "If you're trying to frighten me, you're doing a nice job."

"Good. Someone needs to scare some sense into you."

"Then go to the police with your theory. Let them figure it out. It's what they're supposed to do."

"A job that won't mean much to them. This is very personal to me. Besides, as you just pointed out, I don't have any concrete proof something has happened."

She gestured with her fork. "Exactly. In my profession, I deal with facts, Dr. Collier, as you're supposed to in yours."

He took a bite of his quesadilla. "It's facts you want? Number one, both of our grandfathers died weeks apart, mine supposedly from natural causes, yours from an accident. There are ways to stop a person's heart that appear natural. And there are ways to make something seem like an accident when it isn't. Number two, both of their houses, and Granddad's room at the home, were trashed right after their deaths. Number three, you were followed by someone last night. Number four, our grandfathers have a past that connects them to an archaeological treasure that has never been found, and could be worth millions." Intensity vibrated in his voice as his eyes bored into her.

Maggie felt as though they were the only two people in the whole restaurant, and everything was wiped from her view but him. She was desperate not to believe him, because if what he said was true then her life would change drastically from this moment forward. The unknown lurked before her, prodding her fear to the foreground. She'd battled desperately to remain in control of her life, and that control was slipping away from her.

"Those facts can be explained. Accidents and natural deaths happen all the time. People are robbed all the time. And their connection is almost sixty years old."

He leaned forward. "What about the person who followed you last night? A weirdo out for his jollies?"

"That's a possibility."

Zach shook his head. "You're the most stubborn woman I know. Fine. I tried to warn you of the danger you're in, but it's obvious you're in denial. I'll work on this without your help."

He had tried to understand her position, but he was having a hard time doing it when the facts seemed so obvious. But he couldn't turn his back on her. He wouldn't be able to live with himself if something happened to her, which was why he had returned to the ranch the night before even though he had known it wasn't a wise thing to do.

While Maggie played with her food, not really eating any of her cheese enchiladas, he remembered their confrontation the day before. He should be angry, but that emotion had died quickly. Instead, all he could think about was her long auburn hair, released from its restraints, framing her face in wild disarray while she stood on her grandfather's porch, aiming a shotgun at him. Or her green eyes that were the color of dew-kissed grass. Or her petite frame, just over five feet, that his dwarfed. She was one dynamite-looking woman with one dynamite temper to match.

Taking a bite of his food without really tasting it, he came to a decision. He would give her a few days and then approach her again. She needed time to digest that her grandfather had died, let alone that he might have been murdered. Zach would give her as much time as he could allow, which wasn't much, then he would make her see the truth: *her life was at stake.*

The waitress approached the table. "Would you like dessert?"

"I wouldn't have room for another bite." Maggie smiled at the woman. "The dinner was wonderful."

Her smile was beautiful, Zach thought. It encompassed her whole face, making her eyes shine as if the person receiving it were the only important one around.

Great! That was all he needed to do. Become attracted to a woman who was off-limits. He agreed with her. A Collier and a Somers together would make both their grandfathers turn over in their graves.

Zach tossed his napkin on the table. "I'll take you back to your car."

After paying, he rose and allowed Maggie to walk ahead. He foresaw another restless night, trying to get her out of his mind. It didn't sit well with him that she wouldn't accept his help. If anything happened to her, he would have a hard time not blaming himself.

Outside, the night air, laced with spring, wrapped him in warmth. Before climbing into his car, Zach paused to view the lights of Albuquerque below him. He loved this part of the country, but it had taken his partner's betrayal to get him to move here from Dallas. As a child he used to come every summer to see his grandparents, and he would treasure those memories forever. His heart twisted with the thought that he would never see his grandfather again. Anger pushed through the pain and stiffened his resolve to get to the bottom of his granddad's murder. He might not have proof, but he'd learned to listen to his instincts long ago.

"It's beautiful, isn't it?"

Her voice, with a husky timbre, penetrated his thoughts. "Yes, I have a home not too far from here. I love this view. Sometimes I just wish I had more time to appreciate it. I spend more time at the college than my house."

"That sounds like me. Work can have a way of consuming a person's life."

Over the top of his car, he looked at her. "Do you enjoy your work as a doctor?" He knew a lot about her, having done some research before approaching her with his theory.

She nodded. "And you?"

"Yes."

As he slid behind the steering wheel and started the engine, Maggie settled into her seat. He pulled out of the parking space, the silence between them comfortable, which surprised him after their tense dinner. As he negotiated the first set of curves on the mountain road, the Corvette picked up speed. He pressed his foot on the brake. Nothing. He pumped the brake again. Still nothing.

The car's speed increased. He took the next curve too fast, slamming Maggie against her door. The passenger side scraped the guardrail—the only thing that stood in the way of them and the bottom of the mountain.

Father, I'm in Your hands, he prayed silently.

"What's wrong?"

He didn't need to see the panic on Maggie's face. He could hear it in her voice. Another curve loomed ahead. "Brace yourself. We're in for a rough ride."

FOUR

Maggie latched on to the door handle, her grip so tight that her hand ached. Transfixed, she watched as Zach maneuvered the car around another curve. Each time he put his foot on the brake, nothing happened. Instead, the Corvette kept going faster.

"Do you have your seat belt on?" His voice held a razor-sharp tension.

Her hand trembled as she checked to make sure. "Yes."

"Good. I'm going to try and slow us down as much as possible. If my memory serves me right, there's a field near the bottom that's pretty flat, right off the side of the road. Even if we make it there, Maggie, it's going to be a bumpy ride."

She tensed. The sound of metal grinding against metal thundered in her ears. Every muscle locked into place as the rugged terrain along the side of the road jarred her. Their speed decelerated when they hit a patch of level road, but not enough. Then the asphalt descended again down the side of the mountain.

A hundred things flew through her mind—regrets, wishes. There was so much she hadn't done yet. She didn't have anyone who really cared if she died here at the bottom of one of the steep ravines. The loss of her grandfather deluged her all over again.

Why, Lord? What are You doing?

Maggie saw the field Zach had mentioned up ahead. She held her breath as the car barreled off the road and over the rutted ground. Even with her grip on the door handle and her other hand on the console, she was tossed about. Her knee hit the dashboard. Her head snapped back. Pain raced up her leg and down her spine as the car slowed its speed, then came to an abrupt halt in a shallow ditch, throwing Maggie forward. Her seat belt cut across her chest and stole her breath.

Maggie straightened and pried her hand loose from the handle. Her heartbeat raced, and her breath came out in pants. *Safe. Alive.*

A moan pervaded the pounding in her ears, and she angled around to see if Zach was all right. Slowly he lifted his head from the steering wheel as he reached up to touch his forehead.

The growing darkness prevented her from seeing him well. "Are you okay?"

He didn't answer.

She had been trained not to panic in an emergency, but in the back of her mind she realized how close they had come to dying. She wouldn't let herself think about that now. There would be time later.

Ignoring the part of herself that would like to fall apart, she shoved her door open a few inches until the light came on. Then she turned to Zach to see how serious his injuries were. Blood trickled down his cheek as he stared at a point beyond the car.

"Zach," she whispered, and gently touched his chin to bring his face around for her inspection.

He blinked, then finally focused his attention on her as she probed the gash above his right eye. Not too deep. She tried to maintain her professional facade, but their brush with death had left her vulnerable, stripped of her usual control. Her fingers on his forehead quivered.

"Will I live, Doc?" A huskiness edged his voice.

"Afraid so." She dropped her hand away from him. The trembling spread to encompass her whole body. "I don't even think this will require stitches. You should go to the hospital, though, in case you have a concussion."

"No. I'll be fine." He reached back and pulled a T-shirt from a gym bag and mopped the blood from his face. "Believe me, I've suffered a lot worse than a bump on my forehead."

The finality in his voice erased all arguments from Maggie's lips. "Will you at least let me check you out—" she glanced about "—in better conditions?"

"Sure, later." He tossed the bloodied shirt into the backseat. "But first, I'd like to get out of here."

"Well, just in case you haven't noticed, your car isn't going anywhere."

Zach withdrew his cell from his pocket and punched in a series of numbers. "Ray, Zach here. Can you pick me and a friend up? We've been in an accident."

Maggie half listened as Zach gave his friend directions to where they were. Only for a few seconds had she glimpsed any vulnerability in him. He had just saved their lives with some spectacular driving, and now he was calmly taking charge, getting them a ride, calling a tow truck to pick up his car, as if brake failure were an everyday occurrence for him. Did anything get to this man? She watched him as he made his last call to the police. He was very much in control of his emotions, while she shivered from a cold that had nothing to do with the temperature.

If he ever loved someone, he would demand all of her because he didn't invest himself easily. Whoa, where in the world had that observation come from? She was more shook up than she originally thought if she was putting Zach and love together in the same sentence.

Maggie ignored his words, but tuned in to the sound of his voice. It was rough and warm, slightly gritty, with an indisputable maleness to it that reflected the man. It was the reassuring voice of a person who was used to being in command, to making difficult decisions, possibly even involving dangerous matters. Suddenly a calmness descended on Maggie as though some of his strength had invaded her, soothing her.

"C'mon. Let's wait near the road for Ray." Zach tried his door, but it wouldn't budge. He threw her a grin. "I guess I'll use yours."

She pushed on hers, but it didn't move more than the few inches it was already open. "I think we're stuck."

"Here, let me see." He reached across her body to shove at the door.

His clean, fresh scent overwhelmed her as he pressed against her. Her pulse reacted, racing through her as fast as they had driven down the mountain. His face, inches from hers, held her enthralled. She saw the tiny laugh lines at the corners of his eyes, the gleam that glittered in the gray depths. Her throat went dry.

An eternity later, the door gave way, and he twisted around so he looked directly at her. A connection, forged from a shared near-death experience, mesmerized her, binding them together. That realization should have panicked her, but for a few minutes it didn't. It felt right—a Somers linked with a Collier.

Zach lifted his hand and grazed a finger down her cheek. He started to say something, but a car rounded the curve. A pair of headlights illuminated the ditch in front of them, and sent Zach back to his side of the car. While the vehicle passed them on the road, he gripped the steering wheel, his knuckles white.

She resisted the urge to touch where his finger had. But his effect on her staggered her. A Collier was a taker, not a giver. Those were words she had heard many times from Gramps. She needed to remember them.

Without a word, Maggie stood on shaky legs, clasping the door to steady herself while Zach crawled over the seat and climbed out. He, too, grasped the car, his body so near that the hairs on her arm tingled.

"Are you sure you're all right?" she asked, needing to keep herself focused on being a doctor rather than a woman.

"I told you, I'm fine." He released his grip. "When Ray comes, I think we should go to my place." Before she could protest, he put his finger over her lips. "I don't think this was an accident. That's why I called the police. I want your car checked tomorrow before you drive it back to Santa Fe."

Although she tried to ignore the feel of his touch against her mouth, it took her a long moment to gather her thoughts enough to say, "I can't. I have patients to see first thing in the morning."

Zach didn't say anything. For the next fifteen minutes he went over the details of the accident with a police officer who had arrived and parked at the side of the road. The policeman had a few questions for Maggie, which she answered.

She held her arms close to her chest, but still the cold seeped into her bones. In the middle of the conversation, Zach walked to his trunk and withdrew a jacket. He placed it over Maggie's shoulders, rubbing her arms up and down for a long moment. She wanted to lean back into his strength, to wipe the last hour from her mind, but the officer still had questions for them.

By the time Ray Parker pulled up, followed by the tow truck, Maggie was freezing even with the jacket on. Her teeth chattered, her body quaked. Finished with the police, Zach dealt quickly with the driver of the tow truck, then marshaled Maggie into his friend's Ford Ranger. Zach introduced her to Ray, an associate at the college. She smiled her greeting, still too upset to say more than what was necessary.

In the front seat, Zach drew her against him, his arm about her. His warmth slowly chased the cold away the farther from the accident they went.

"What happened back there?" Ray slanted a glance at Zach.

"I'm not sure, other than the brakes failed at a crucial time."

"You don't think this has anything to do with Red's death, do you?"

"Yes."

That one word brought back all the distressing thoughts that Maggie had had over the past twenty-four hours. *Robbery. Attempted murder. Murder.* She wasn't equipped to deal with those kinds of things. She was a healer. Caught between denial and seeking answers, she didn't know what to do next. She needed time to think, to figure out how best to proceed.

Gramps murdered? Over the diary? Why now?

As Ray pulled up in front of what she assumed was Zach's house, her head felt as though a jackhammer pounded against her skull. Her muscles ached, especially her neck, as if she had climbed the stairs to a fifty-story building. And the second Zach disengaged himself from her, the cold burrowed deeper into her bones. That reaction scared her. His presence was taking over her life. She didn't give up control easily, if ever, to another human being. Even with the Lord she'd struggled with that.

"Come in, Ray. I need a favor." Zach slipped from the cab. He offered Maggie his hand. For a long second she stared at it, almost afraid of what it would symbolize if she put hers in his. She'd always stood on her own two feet and not depended on another person, not even Gramps. She couldn't allow herself to do it now, because the situation was complicated, possibly dangerous and definitely unusual.

Resisting his assistance, she climbed from the truck and pulled the jacket about her to ward off the cold. Zach stared at her for a moment, his arm dropping to his side.

As she trudged up the walk toward Zach's adobe-style house, disquiet crackled in the air. Her knee throbbed where she'd hit the dashboard. Pain radiated from her neck, across her shoulders and down her back.

Inside, Zach flipped on a switch and light flooded his large, open living room, with its high ceiling. Masculine touches stamped the place, with Indian artifacts on the walls and tables. More like a museum, she thought as she surveyed the area before her. Any other time she would have appreciated his beautiful Indian art—collected from around the world, not just the United States—but at the moment the only thing she wanted to do was sleep for a week and forget what had happened.

Zach waved her toward a brown suede couch. "Sit. Do you want something to drink? Coffee? Soda? Tea?"

"No, I'm afraid I'd never go to sleep if I had any caffeine." She wasn't even sure she could fall asleep if she didn't have it. But she knew if she didn't sleep soon she wouldn't be able to function for long, let alone figure out what was going on.

"Ray, anything to drink?"

Zach's friend shook his head.

Zach took the chair across from Maggie while Ray sat at the other end of the sofa. Silence ruled for a few minutes. Maggie laced her fingers to keep them from quivering. As a doctor, she'd dealt with emergencies before, but they had always involved others. This one she was very much in the middle of. Memories of a time when she was thirteen taunted her. She pushed away thoughts of the past. She couldn't go there.

"You're safe here." A hardness entered Zach's gaze as it found hers. "I won't let anything happen to you."

"*Safe?* I'm not sure what that word means anymore." But his declaration had for a moment alleviated what panic and fear still resided in her.

"Are you sure you want to be alone tonight?"

"I have a friend I can call. Don't worry about me." *I'll do that enough for the both of us.* "She lives down the street from me."

Zach turned his attention to Ray. "May I borrow your truck to take Maggie back to Santa Fe?"

"Sure. You can just drop me off at home. It's on the way."

"We were lucky tonight." Although Zach's comment was directed at his friend, his gaze fastened on Maggie.

Ray frowned. "This is getting serious. Have you talked to the police?"

"We did tonight, but there isn't much to go on. We won't know why the brakes failed until tomorrow, when a mechanic looks at them. But I don't need a mechanic to tell me they were tampered with." His hard tone underscored each word of his last sentence.

"You aren't thinking of going after these guys yourself, are you?" Ray sat forward, resting his elbows on his knees.

"You have a better suggestion?"

"Yes. Let the police do their job. Stay out of it."

"I would, but someone is after the codices, and the police don't have the time to look for whoever it is."

"And you do? What about the expedition you're planning for next month when the semester is over? We have the backers coming into town in a few days. They want to meet with you. There's still a lot we need to do. Besides, you've got classes to teach."

"This is important. I'll make the time. You could always cover for me if the need arose. And I won't miss the reception for the expedition backers."

"Yes, but—" Ray snapped his mouth closed. "Forget it. I know that look. You aren't going to give up until you learn the truth."

"No, I'm not. Granddad is dead because of the codices. They are the key to what's going on."

The steel determination in Zach's voice sent a tremor down Maggie's spine. This man across from her was very capable of taking care of himself—and her, if she let him. She hoped they were on the same side, that he didn't have a secret agenda concerning the Aztec codices and treasure. It was even possible there were three sides to this—Zach's, hers and someone else's.

"The expedition to the Amazon is important. Don't forget that. I'll do what I can to help, but you're still the one heading it. The backers are funding it because of that." Ray rose. "I think I do want something to drink." When Zach made a move toward the kitchen, his friend said, "Sit. Rest. I know my way around. I'll get it."

When his associate left them alone, Maggie said, "He knows about the codices. Who else have you told?"

"He was with me when I discovered the break-in at my grandfather's. I never told him about the diary." He leaned closer and lowered his voice to a whisper. "Nor the fact I have a copy of the map."

"Before you take me home, let me look at your head." She needed to put space between them, but the doctor in her wouldn't let her not offer to check out his cut.

"I'm fine." Zach waved her off and started to stand.

"I seem to remember you telling me you'd let me look at you later. Well, for your information, later is here. Now."

Coming to his feet, Zach towered over her. His gaze trapped hers. She found herself rising and standing so close to him that his scent surrounded her. Her heartbeat surged.

"Are you all right? I noticed you limping a little," he said.

His tender look trekked down to her parched throat. She swallowed several times before answering, "I'm fine, and this little diversion won't change my mind. I want to check you out before we leave." She forced a lightness into her voice, even though the situation between them was quickly becoming serious, the connection they shared strengthening.

He smiled. "You can't blame a guy for trying. I've never been fond of going to the doctor."

"I've heard that before," she said with a laugh. "Doesn't change my mind. Do you have a first-aid kit?"

"Yes, I'll get it."

Light-headed, Maggie lowered herself onto the couch. Until he'd left the room, she hadn't realized she hadn't taken a decent breath since they had faced each other. Inhaling deeply now, she scanned the living room, trying to get a sense of the man who had taken over her life so effectively in the past day.

The colors of the room were the tan of the desert and the green of the barrel cactus. Beneath her feet was a beautifully woven Navajo Indian rug, worth a small fortune. The room was neat and orderly, much like her house except hers had a lived-in look while his didn't. She got the impression he was rarely home. Again she thought of a museum as her regard took in his possessions.

"Okay, let's get this over with." Zach sat next to her and gave her the first-aid kit. "Did I mention I hate going to the doctor?"

"Yes. Too bad."

She managed to block from her mind to whom she attended as she checked his gash, cleaned it then placed a bandage over it. If she hadn't been able to block him from her mind, she was sure she would have been in trouble. Zach Collier was just too much for her to handle at this time in her life. She had everything mapped out for herself. Her career and new practice were what was most important at the moment. She had spent years becoming a doctor, with she and her grandfather both making sacrifices to pay for medical school. Maybe in a few years, when she was more established, she could think about something other than being a doctor. Who was she kidding? She knew the real reason she didn't focus on her personal life, and it had nothing to do with her profession. How long was she going to let what had happened between her and Brad Wentworth dictate what she did with her life?

"Well, what's the verdict, Doc?"

"Oh, I'd say at least another fifty thousand miles." She shoved thoughts of Brad back into the far reaches of her mind.

"That's comforting, since this bod may get a lot of wear and tear in the near future."

"You really are going to pursue this?" She looked him directly in the eye.

"Yes." All the tenderness in his expression vanished, and a ruthless determination appeared in its place. "To the end, Maggie. I won't let these people get away with what they did to our grandfathers."

She wanted to believe him in that moment—almost did. Except, for over thirty years she had been raised to hate, and especially never to trust, anyone with the last name Collier. There was a small part of her that still doubted him even after the brake failure. She felt that if she believed him she was betraying Gramps. "How will you pursue it, Zach?"

Raking his hand through his hair, he rose to prowl the room. "I don't know yet. Maybe I'll find the clue in the map, after all."

"But you said your grandfather studied it for years and could never find the answer."

"I know. He thought he could break the code. If those people hadn't gotten the diary, we might be able to figure out the mystery of the codices."

She busied herself putting the bandages and medicine back into the first-aid kit, while the scent of coffee drifted toward her. Something was going on. She didn't doubt that anymore. But she had no idea who was behind it. It could still be Zach. The one thing she did know was that she wasn't equipped to solve the mystery of the codices by herself. If anything was going to be done, it would have to be done as a team.

A team. The words vibrated in her mind, conjuring up images of she and Zach working closely together, his thoughts hers, his actions a perfect mirror of hers. A warmth suffused her and made her hands quiver as she closed the lid on the kit and set it on the end table.

I hope I'm not making a big mistake. She inhaled a deep breath to fortify herself and said, "Zach, I have something to tell you."

He stopped pacing and faced her. Although his expression became unreadable, his body grew taut.

"I have the diary," she whispered. She clutched the arm of the couch and waited for his wrath.

He closed the space between them, his gaze straying toward the kitchen. "Where?" The deadly quiet of his voice unnerved her more than if he had shouted the question.

"My grandfather gave it to me on my thirtieth birthday. I used to keep it in my armoire."

"Used to?"

She hated the way he stared at her with no emotion in his features, in his voice. "This afternoon, before I came to Albuquerque, I put it in a safety-deposit box."

He turned toward the door. "Let's go."

"Where?"

"I'm taking you home. There isn't anything more we can do tonight."

"What about the diary? I thought you wanted it."

He whipped around to confront her, his expression no longer blank but full of fury, all directed at her. "What do you suggest I do? Break into the bank to get it?"

"No."

He walked back to her. "Do you want me to applaud you for being such a good liar? I actually believed they had the journal."

The full force of his rage bombarded her—although his voice had never risen above a whisper—as he came to a halt in front of her. She released her grip on the arm of the couch and craned her neck upward until their gazes clashed. "I didn't lie," she said. "The diary wasn't at my grandfather's."

"Oh, I see. You like to play word games." He invaded her space completely, hovering over her. "What other games do you like to play?"

The fire of her anger matched his as she stood so he wouldn't have the advantage of height—well, at least not as badly as when she sat. "Just when I thought there could be more to a Collier than Gramps thought, you've taken care of any delusions on my part. Why do you think I kept it a secret? Do you think I'm stupid enough to hand it over to you with no questions asked? Colliers take. You obviously fit the mold, like Red."

His cold eyes narrowed, holding an intensity that she had never encountered before. His dark, hawklike features twisted into a grimace that iced her blood. "If you're comparing me to my grandfather, then I accept the compliment. And, yes, I do take what I want. If you're not willing to fight for your beliefs, then you'll always be dissatisfied with life. I wouldn't want to end up a bitter old man who lives in the past."

His contemptuous words, directed at her grandfather, struck low and hard, choking off her next breath. "And in the process forget honor? The ends justify the means? Is that the Collier motto?"

"One thing is obvious. Your grandfather's account of the past is quite different from my grandfather's."

"The difference is the difference between the truth and lies."

The rigidity in his lean, contorted frame transmitted the force of his fury. "I can see I was wrong to think we could work together on this."

"All you want from me is the diary. Nothing else matters."

He stared into her eyes for a long, suspended moment, his gaze an almost physical touch. "Believe what you want. I don't care." He strode toward the entry hall. "I'll drive you home now. Ray, we need to leave," he shouted toward the kitchen.

All emotions were gone from his voice as he opened the front door and waited for her and his friend to exit. Maggie walked beside Ray, who held a mug of coffee. Zach locked his house then followed, staying ten feet behind them.

"Where it involves his granddad, he feels strongly." Zach's friend said, then sipped his hot drink.

"So, you heard." Did Ray know about the diary now?

"Some. I thought it best to hide out in the kitchen until things calmed down."

"Wise." But Zach and she hadn't been wise when they had let their tempers get the better of them. How much had they revealed to Ray concerning the existence of the journal?

Zach said nothing to her when he finally slid into the cab and drove to Ray's house to drop off his friend. On the hour-long trip to Santa Fe, the silence eroded her spurt of anger. She realized that if they wanted to solve the mystery they would have to work together, even with neither trusting the other completely. They couldn't do it alone. Each had half of the puzzle—if the legend was to be believed.

On the outskirts of the town, she gave Zach directions to her house, still no closer to deciding whether to give him the diary or not. She peered at him, limned against the city lights, his face stern, his shoulders set in grim lines. The play of shadows over his features made him appear implacable, and in that moment she did believe he got what he wanted—always.

When he parked in her driveway, he glared straight ahead while he waited for her to leave. She started to tell him he could have the diary, that she was just too tired and confused to deal with the mystery, but the words wouldn't come out. She remained silent and descended from the cab.

Exhausted, barely able to put one foot in front of the other, she limped to her porch, unlocked her door and stepped inside. She dropped her purse on a console table, then switched on the living-room light by the entrance. She stared at the man before her, all in black, wearing a ski mask. Fear immobilized her momentarily. When she whirled around to run, he leaped on her and roped her to him while his gloved hand clamped her scream in her mouth.

"Well, well, if it isn't the little lady of the house."

FIVE

The hiss of the man's words, accompanied by his garlic-laced breath, paralyzed Maggie with fear, draining what strength she had left. She struggled to drag air into her lungs, to imbue energy into her numb body, but his large black-gloved hand about her mouth and nose cut off her attempts to inhale. Darkness hovered at the edge of her mind, inching closer with each second the man held her trapped against his bulk in the entry hall.

Fight!

She tried to clear the dark mist, to twist away, but her muscles wouldn't respond to the command from her groggy mind. Then the thug's hand slipped slightly lower, allowing oxygen to rush into her lungs for a few precious seconds.

"Where's the diary?" he demanded.

The heat of panic infused the cold dread, crushing her chest and causing a constriction about her that had nothing to do with the man imprisoning her. Zach was gone; she was alone with this goon and the diary wasn't here.

Think!

"I won't have to hurt you if you'll just give it to me." The man began to haul her toward the living room.

Her feet scraped across the tile floor as she went limp in his arms, hoping her deadweight would slow him down. It didn't. She grappled for options. None came to mind.

"Cooperate and you'll live to breathe another day." The threat, spoken next to her ear, chilled her as though she'd plunged into a glacier-filled sea. "Take your hand away," she mumbled into his palm, realizing he wouldn't be able to understand her words. Bile rose in her throat at the taste of his leather glove.

"What?" he demanded. In one fluid motion he spun her around so she faced him, and shoved her up against the wall by the entrance to the living room, while she gasped for air. Then, using his body to pin her against the wood paneling, he clasped his hand over her mouth again. Everything had happened so fast she hadn't had time to react, to scream.

"What did you say?" He pressed himself into her, a sneer—as though he took pleasure in intimidating her—appearing through the slit where his mouth was.

All she saw was his white teeth flash, and his blue eyes, the color of a periwinkle, glitter with malice. She lowered her gaze to his fingers, still over her mouth. "Take your hand away," she mumbled again with all the force she could muster.

"You try anything, you'll regret it." He eased the pressure on her mouth, wariness clouding his gaze. "So, where is the diary?"

Go for the eyes. She remembered that from some article she'd read on self-defense.

She wilted against the wall as though she had no energy left to remain standing. He automatically went to hold her up. She gulped in a deep breath, then screamed, the sound ripped from her gut. At the same time she shoved at his massive weight and jammed her fingers toward his eyes, striking one, missing the other.

The thug cursed. He jerked her hands down and slammed her up against the paneling. Her head hit it with a thud. Dazed, she blinked. The watery blue of his eyes, then his snarling teeth, came into view in the black sea of his mask.

"You like to play rough?"

The sinister questions slithered down her like a serpent. Drawing on a well of hidden strength, she thrashed and flailed, struggling to break free of his ironclad hold. Her feeble attempts did nothing but cause the man to mash himself into her, flattening her against the wall until she couldn't breathe.

His hideous laughter ricocheted around in her mind like a bullet gone haywire. His garlic breath assaulted her senses, jamming a choking lump in her throat.

"Gonna fight me? That's okay. I like to play rough, too. Adds some excitement to a dull, routine job."

Dull, routine job? She wanted to laugh hysterically at the man's description of what he was doing. But that irrational impulse quickly fled, to be replaced with sheer terror. It leaked through the haze that blanketed her mind.

"I brought Betsy with me for just this kind of thing.

Don't go anywhere without my knife." One hand released her arm while the other continued to press into her mouth.

She looked down and saw him fumbling in his pocket. *Oh, no!* She squeezed her eyes shut, feeling trapped, as if she were in a cave-in, with tons of rocks on top of her and no way to escape.

The blare of the doorbell sliced into the air. Her eyes bolted open.

Her assailant glanced toward the front door. When the bell rang again, he shifted his bulk slightly, his fingers still in his jeans pocket. The movement eased the pressure on her mouth. She bit down on the pad of his other hand. He jerked away as his gaze flew back to her face. She screamed and shoved at him. He slapped her, knocking her head to the side. Pain swirled in the dark corners of her mind.

In the next instant, the front door burst open and crashed against the wall. The thug finished pulling the switchblade from his pocket as he swiveled to meet the new threat entering the house. Maggie scrambled away before the thug decided to use her as a human shield. Her attention fastened on to Zach Collier, who filled her foyer with his large presence. She had never been so thankful to see someone before.

"Okay?" Zach asked Maggie, while he kept his attention trained on the man between her and himself.

"Yes," she mumbled through lips that already felt swollen from the blow. Trying to ignore the throbbing ache where she had been struck, she worked her jaw, then wiped a trickle of blood from her chin with her finger.

Not once did Zach's gaze stray from the goon who was as tall as he was, fifty pounds heavier and with his knife in hand. Zach eyed the man as though gauging his prowess. The metal of the blade caught the light and glinted.

Suddenly Maggie's assailant rushed toward Zach. She gasped. Zach kicked at the arm that held the knife, and the blade went sailing from the thug, clanging across the tiles in the entrance, toward the hallway to the bedrooms. For a few seconds the man paused, weaponless. Then he continued forward, barreling into Zach in the middle of the foyer. They flew across the entry hall and thundered against the far wall. A picture fell to the floor at the same time the two men did, the crashing sound vying with their grunts.

She needed to call the police. She rushed to the phone and snatched it up. No dial tone. She tossed the plastic receiver down and looked about for her purse with her cell phone in it. Then she remembered it was in the foyer, on the table by the front door where she'd dropped it when she'd come in.

Against the backdrop of the sounds of the scuffle, Maggie frantically scanned the living room behind her for any kind of weapon she could use on the assailant. When she spied a vase close by, she hurried to it. A groan from Zach urged her to move faster as she clasped the piece of porcelain and spun toward the fight, now close to the door.

Zach was on top, and he pummeled his fist into the man's face. The thug moaned and bucked, causing them to roll again. They banged into a table in the foyer, sending Maggie's purse falling to the floor. Its contents scattered across the tiles.

While the thug hovered over Zach, Maggie rushed forward with her "weapon" in hand. Then suddenly Zach pushed against the man, and their positions switched yet again. Frustrated, she put the vase down, afraid she would do more harm than good.

But she had to do something before Zach got hurt. The grunts and moans coming from the men propelled her toward her cell, which had slid across the tile floor. She started to punch in 9-1-1 when she realized her battery was dead. Her frustration mounted with each second of impotency.

She pivoted toward the two men. Standing now, arms outstretched, they both slowly moved in a wide circle in the foyer. A cut on Zach's lip bled, along with the gash from the accident, since the bandage had ripped off during the fight. Her attacker's mouth was split and blood soaked his ski mask.

"Who sent you?" Zach asked, his voice menacingly quiet in the silence of the house.

The man grinned, but a coldness remained in his blue eyes. "I'm no fool. If I told you, I'm a dead man."

"Who sent you?" Zach asked again.

Maggie hadn't thought it possible that Zach's voice could get any more deadly, but it did. She took in his alert, predatory gleam, his rage packed in ice, and shuddered.

The thug managed to sidestep until his booted foot touched his switchblade. He swooped down and picked the knife up, tossing it to his other hand. "Maybe I should be the one to ask the questions. Where's the diary?"

"You'll get it over my dead body," Maggie said.

"Then so be it."

Her attacker lunged forward. Maggie screamed, momentarily startling him. With his attention diverted to her, he missed Zach by several inches. Zach dodged the man and came up behind him, locking his fingers around the assailant's wrist.

Zach's mouth slashed into a scowl, his eyes a blaze of steel fury. "Drop it or I'll break your wrist."

Behind his mask, the man chortled. He brought his elbow back into Zach's stomach, and a swish of air left Zach's lungs. Maggie started edging toward the vase again. Maybe this time she could do something.

Sucking in deeply, Zach backed away from the man. The goon spun around, and they faced off. The man taunted Zach with his knife, waving it in front of him. Maggie's fingers closed around the vase as their assailant flipped the switchblade and sent it sailing toward Zach. He dived to the side. The knife landed with a clang on the tile floor a foot from Maggie in the entrance to the living room. The vase crashed to the floor.

She looked down at the blade among the shards of porcelain, then back up at her attacker. Seeing she was closest to the only weapon, the man whirled around and raced for the door as Maggie lunged toward the blade.

Zach staggered to his feet and followed the thug outside. His footsteps pounding the ground matched the pounding of his heart as he ran after the man. Zach wanted to get his hands around the intruder's neck. Maggie's assailant was ten yards ahead. Zach increased his speed, determined to make him pay for every second of fear he had given Maggie. Eight yards. Six.

With his chest burning, each breath a painful exertion, Zach closed the gap between himself and the huge man. For a few seconds the man disappeared around the corner. Vigilant, not relenting, Zach hurried after him. As he came around the hedge, Zach saw the man dive for the open passenger door of a black SUV.

Zach put every ounce of strength into the last few yards, leaping for the closing door. It slammed shut the same instant the vehicle shrieked away from the curb. Zach landed on his knees with a wrenching jolt as the SUV sped away. Pain bolted up his thighs and he fell forward, planting his hands in the thick, cool grass in front of him.

Dragging in shallow breaths, he tried to read the license tag, but all he could see was one number, a four. The rest were covered up with caked-on mud.

Slowly he stood. His hands curled and uncurled at his sides. *Father, forgive me. For a moment I wanted to kill.* Never before had he felt such powerless rage at another person than when he saw the assailant's hands on Maggie.

Maggie!

He had to get back to her. Ignoring the pain in his knees, he jogged to her house, all the while scanning the terrain in case the people in the black SUV decided to return. The stakes were getting higher and higher with each day that passed. And he and Maggie were caught in the middle.

When he entered her house, his rage, like a cut that

refused to heal, festered anew at the sight of the destruction. Before facing her, he paused in the entryway and gathered his calm about him, bending over to inhale gulps of air.

When he walked into the living room, Maggie glanced toward him. The glare of the lamp accentuated the paleness of her features and brought out the red marks of the man's hands on her neck and face. The haunting crystalline green of her eyes spoke of her terror more than any words could. Her auburn hair, a tangled mess about her, attracted his gaze before his eyes finally settled on her swollen lips.

His chest constricted. He fought the rise of fury and concentrated instead on Maggie's needs. He crossed the room and paused in front of her.

She lifted her gaze to his. Her hand trembled as she ran it through her hair. For a long moment silence reigned, then the urge to hold her, to make sure she was all right, took over. He gathered her to him and cushioned her cheek against him.

Safe. For the time being. Maggie slid her eyes closed and relished that fleeting feeling. She heard Zach's heartbeat beneath her ear, and the sound further comforted her, its rhythmic pace as soothing as if she were listening to rushing water over rocks.

While he stroked the length of her back, her mind refused to think beyond the consoling sensations of his hand. He was a man who was very capable of protecting her. Her thoughts went blank. The tremors slowly subsided inside her, as though he brushed away her fear with each caress.

"Maggie, we need to get out of here. They may return."

His whispered words tickled her ear, bringing her back to the moment, to the reality of what had happened in her home, her sanctuary. "They?" she managed to ask around the lump in her throat.

He pulled back. "The man jumped into a getaway car. Someone else was driving."

There are at least two, maybe more, after me. That distressing realization shattered what was left of her composure. She wanted to move, to do what he said, but she felt rooted to the floor.

"Maggie? We've got to leave now." He took her hand and tugged her toward the entrance into the living room.

She stared at the strong fingers wrapped around hers, as if she were watching the scene from above, and the woman moving in slow motion wasn't her. Sluggishly she raised her head and looked into his eyes. His worried expression produced a tightly aching dryness in her throat. She swallowed hard several times. She shuddered, a trickle of feeling welling upward like the beginning of a stream.

"Are you okay?" he asked.

She nodded.

In the foyer he paused in front of her. She fought the warmth spreading through her as his hands slid up her arms. She didn't want to remember the panic and terror of moments before, the sense that her life wasn't hers anymore—as in the cave years ago. She'd worked hard all her life never to feel that way again.

Zach cupped her face and smiled down at her, his

thumbs stirring over her cheeks in slow circles. "I won't let anything happen to you. I'll find someplace safe for us tonight and come up with a plan tomorrow."

"I've never…had someone attack…" Words failed her. She wanted to talk about what had occurred, but she couldn't put it into a coherent sentence. So much had happened in the past day. Too much. Too fast.

His hands rested on her shoulders. The savage twist to his mouth attested to his emotions as he kneaded her taut muscles. "No one will attack you if I can do anything to prevent it. That's a promise. We'll find out who's behind this and stop them."

Maggie closed her eyes to the comforting feel of his hands on her, stroking away her agitation with his touch. She wanted to lean into him, but she had already depended on him for so much. In the past she had always stood on her own two feet, never depending on another person—not even Gramps, her mentor. The Southwest, a land that was often harsh and barren, had long ago taught her she had to rely on herself if she was to survive its realities.

Opening her eyes, she drew on her inner strength. "I'm fine." When he threw her a questioning look, she added, "Really, I am, Zach."

"Okay. Pack a few things. I don't think you should stay here until we've figured this out."

Against Zach's protests, Maggie tended to his cuts, her movements quick and efficient. She gave him some aspirin and took some herself. Tomorrow her body would protest the assailant's harsh treatment of her.

Then, with Zach's help, Maggie packed an overnight bag. She was aware he thought the man might return with reinforcements, and she only took what was necessary. Five minutes later, she sat in Ray's black truck while Zach headed away from her house. She looked back at her home, which had been her haven. She wasn't sure she would ever feel safe there again, and hated that her attacker had taken her sanctuary away.

As Zach drove out of Santa Fe, Maggie could think of nothing to say, her thoughts still a jumbled mess. She'd always prided herself on being logical and orderly, both necessary traits in her profession, but right now she couldn't put any kind of logical order to her thoughts, and gave up trying. That would come later.

Except for an occasional light dotting the landscape, pitch-black was all Maggie saw around her when Zach pulled off the highway and bumped along a dirt road that led to a house. *Am I making a mistake putting my trust in him?* He'd said they were going somewhere safe, to stay with a cousin who lived on a reservation. But what if this was all an elaborate setup to get the diary?

For miles she hadn't seen many signs of life. If Gramps knew who she was with— She quaked thinking how angry her grandfather would have been.

Everything she'd done in her life had been for Gramps. He'd taken her in after her mother's death, only a year after her father had died in the cave-in. Gramps had held her when she had cried for her parents at night. He'd cheered her on when she had decided to become a doctor. He'd made sacrifices so she could achieve her goal. She owed him, and this was definitely not the way to repay her grandfather. Guilt gnawed at her composure, which was pieced together with a fragile thread.

"Your cousin doesn't mind us dropping in?" Maggie asked, not liking where her thoughts were taking her.

"Evelyn's home is always open to family. I have a lot of cousins in this area. If someone is checking out my relatives, it will take them a while. Besides, one of my cousins is a tribal police officer. Nothing much happens without him knowing about it."

In the dark she sensed the brush of his glance.

"Both Evelyn and Hawke are very knowledgeable about the terrain in this part of the country. That might prove useful to us when looking for the codices."

"I see." His relatives were Willow-in-the-Wind's family, the woman her grandfather had been engaged to marry before Red Collier had run off with her.

Zach parked behind the house so the black truck couldn't be seen from the road, then climbed from the cab while she grabbed her overnight bag and exited, too. Several more lights in the house switched on, as though someone was moving toward the back door. When it opened, an older woman, medium height with long, straight, coal-black hair, stood in the entrance. Her face lit with a smile as she saw Zach coming toward her.

"Twice in one month. What do I owe this visit to?" The woman stepped out onto the small stoop.

Zach enveloped her in a hug. "We need a safe place to stay for a few days."

The woman pulled back and studied him. "Trouble?"

Maggie approached the pair while Zach turned toward her and said, "Evelyn Lonechief, this is Maggie Somers." He scanned the darkness beyond the pool of light created by the house. "And I'll explain inside why we're here."

"Come in." His cousin opened the screen door and went into the kitchen.

Maggie mounted the two steps, and again the feeling she was consorting with the enemy nudged to the foreground. Too dazed by the attack at her house, she hadn't questioned Zach about where they were going until they were halfway here.

"I'll put some coffee on." Evelyn shuffled toward the counter.

Just inside the doorway Maggie surveyed the kitchen, a small refrigerator and a stove the only modern conveniences. A dark brown rectangular table with six chairs around it dominated the middle of the room. Old, cream-colored linoleum covered the floor. The room oozed warmth, as though it was the heart of the house.

As the scent of brewing coffee permeated the air, Evelyn lowered herself into one of the chairs and waited for Maggie and Zach to take a seat. "Hawke should be home soon."

Zach slid a look toward Maggie. "That's my cousin who's a tribal police officer, and Evelyn's son."

"So what kind of trouble are you in this time?"

Surprised by the question, Maggie stared at Zach. She knew about the problem in the Amazon last year, but what else?

Evelyn chuckled. "Zach has a habit of finding trouble. You should get him to tell you about that time in Peru. Or remember when you went to the Philippines a few years back? I still marvel about how you got out of that situation alive."

No wonder Maggie had gotten the impression he could take care of himself, she thought. *He's had to, whereas the extent of my adventures has been the last two days.*

Evelyn's dark features brightened. "He's a regular Indiana Jones. Made Red proud. If Zach wasn't looking for some new plant or cure, he was delving into the local history. Sometimes people didn't want him to."

Zach shot to his feet. "I'll get us all some coffee, then we'll talk about what's going on."

While he was at the counter, Evelyn leaned toward Maggie. "He doesn't like me talking about his adventures, but I sure do enjoy hearing about them. It's my excitement. Nothing much happens around here."

"Glad to hear that." Maggie took the mug Zach gave her and sipped the hot brew. "We have someone after us."

Zach eased down next to her, cradling his coffee between his hands. "Maggie is Jake Somers's granddaughter."

A twinkle sparkled in Evelyn's brown eyes. "I figured as much. She has the same dark red hair and the same mouth. Why your grandfather was called Red is beyond me. It should have been Jake's name."

"You knew my grandfather?"

"I knew who he was, but I never met him. I've seen some old photos of him, heard stories about him. I'm sorry about his death."

Her words of condolence brought back all the pain Maggie had experienced over the past week. "Zach thinks it wasn't an accident, and I have to agree with him."

"Like Red?"

Zach nodded.

"He shared his theory with you?" Maggie glanced from Zach to his cousin.

"With my son, after Red's house was trashed and the map was stolen," Evelyn said.

"And Hawke thinks something might be going on." Zach lifted his mug to his lips, his gaze snagging Maggie's over the rim.

Maggie gave him an exaggerated look. "I believe someone is after us. It's kinda hard not to acknowledge it when I was attacked in my own home."

Evelyn sat forward. "You were attacked? Why?"

"The man wanted the diary." Her attacker's gravelly voice, and his demands, resounded in Maggie's mind. If Zach hadn't come in, she could have been killed.

"So, Zach, your hunch is right. This is about the legend of the Aztec codices, after all these years. Red and Aunt Willow gave up on the search. They decided the codices were either destroyed or the legend was just that, a legend."

"Well, someone docsn't think so." Zach placed his mug on the table.

"Either way, Zach and I are in danger because of the diary and the map. If the codices are out there, we need to find them."

Zach surged to his feet. "They belong in a museum where they can be studied, not in some private collector's possession. The prospects of a band of Aztecs preserving their history from destruction for future generations…" His voice faded, but the passion in his expression didn't.

"You sound just like your grandfather. Why didn't you become an archaeologist like him?" Evelyn finished her coffee.

"It's hard to live up to a legend. I wanted to make my own mark in the scientific community."

Maggie watched Zach pace the kitchen, waves of energy flowing from him. Red Collier had had the life—and woman—Gramps had wanted. Although she felt her grandfather had loved her grandmother in his own way, Maggie had always known something had been missing in their relationship. Red and Jake's discovery almost sixty years ago had started an avalanche of events. Would it end in Maggie's death?

"Did they get the diary, too?" Evelyn walked to the coffeepot and poured some more coffee into her mug.

Zach stopped in the middle of the room. "No. So we have a chance."

Evelyn lounged back against the counter with her drink nestled in her palms. "Which means they will be searching for you and Maggie. If they have already killed twice for the diary and map, then they won't stop until they get both of them."

They? Who are they? Maggie wanted to scream in frustration. She'd had a good life, and now she was on the run, forced to work with her family's enemy in order to stay alive.

SIX

"Are you sure about this?" Maggie scanned the parking lot at the Albuquerque City College, looking for a black SUV with gun-toting thugs in it.

"We'll get the copy of the map, interview the people at the rehabilitation center, go by the bank in Santa Fe and be back at Evelyn's before anyone knows we are here." Zach patted the hood of the green Jeep. "Whoever is after us won't be looking for this rental car. Besides, we're probably going to need a four-wheel drive. I doubt very seriously the codices are hidden in the middle of civilization."

"And there are definitely some remote places in the Southwest where they could be stashed. There are a lot in New Mexico alone."

"But first we need to break the code, figure out where to start looking."

Maggie fell into step next to Zach as he crossed the parking lot toward the science building. Her skin crawled with visions of people watching them. She perused the area, but saw nothing out of the ordinary, no gun-toting thugs waving their arms to get her attention.

Inside, Zach greeted the receptionist with a nod and a smile but kept walking toward his office. The star-struck expression on the young woman's face amused Maggie, while Zach seemed oblivious to his effect on the receptionist. Maggie hurried after him. His long strides chewed up the distance rapidly, as if he was a man on a mission.

"Slow down."

He glanced back at her. "I don't want to stay here any longer than is necessary."

At his office door, she spied the taut line of his mouth. "You felt it, too?"

He nodded, unlocked the door and entered the room.

Maggie quickly followed, not breathing fully until she was inside. "Are we being paranoid, or do you think someone is watching us?"

"I hope the first, but wouldn't be surprised if it's the latter." He walked directly to the bookcase along the south wall and withdrew a large volume from the top shelf. "After yesterday's events, I'm sure they know we're working together."

"And they want to stop that?"

"Yes." He stuck his hand into the vacant hole left by the large book. "I think that's why someone tampered with my brakes. They wanted to get rid of me, or at least scare me off."

"My car was okay."

"They want you alive until they get the journal. They made the mistake of killing your grandfather before they got it. They probably thought it was at his house, as my grandfather's map was. Like yours, my grandfather couldn't part with the artifact and give it to a museum."

Their grandfathers kept the items as a constant reminder of the past. A past that had killed them and could kill her and Zach. Maggie shivered, her mind journeying back to the previous evening, when they'd been barreling down the mountain with no brakes. "I guess they didn't think we would combine forces, or they wouldn't have tried to kill you with me in the car."

He pulled his hand out of the hole in the shelf, a piece of folded paper clutched in it. "I think they did something to the brakes here at the college, or maybe even at my house. The mechanic said the way it was tampered with would cause a slow leak." He waved the copy of the map in the air. "But we're going to be smarter than they are."

Thinking back to the times she had witnessed her grandfather poring over the pages of the diary, and seeing the disappointment carved into his features, she had to suppress the strong urge to snatch the paper from Zach's grip and discover what the big deal was. Then she considered the task ahead of her and Zach, and felt overwhelmed. A treasure. A map. A diary. Breaking some code. This was all beyond her expertise. She was a doctor, not a cryptographer.

"Let's get out of here. We still need to go to the rehabilitation center and then the bank in Santa Fe," he said.

"It's down the street from my office."

Zach stuck the map into his pocket and opened his office door to allow her to go first. She hastened down the corridor. Zach's hand settled at the small of her back, reassuring her of his presence.

When she rounded the corner, she ran into a tall, thin man, his attention fixed on some papers he carried. Her purse, wrenched from her grasp in the collision, fell to the tile floor. All its contents scattered. Stunned for a few seconds, she just stared at the man, who quickly bent to scoop up her bag and items.

"I'm so sorry." Red in the face, the older gentleman stuffed her wallet, checkbook and compact into the purse, then gave it to her. "I should have been looking where I was going." He peered over her shoulder. "Zach, you're just the person I wanted to see."

Zach stepped around her and shook the man's hand. "This is Maggie Somers. John Kingston. He runs the museum at the college and was one of my grandfather's protégés."

John eyed her. "Somers? Any kin to Jake Somers?"

"My grandfather." Surprised the man knew Gramps, Maggie looped the straps of her purse over her shoulder and tucked it under her arm. "How did you know my grandfather?"

"I didn't. I've heard stories from Red." The museum curator's questioning gaze swung to Zach.

Zach held up his hand. "I know. When I have more time, I'll fill you in. Right now we have to be going."

He knew stories of Gramps? Maggie didn't like the idea Red Collier had talked about her grandfather to others.

John frowned. "Is something going on? I know you were upset about the break-in at Red's place."

"I'm sure it was someone looking for an easy score," Zach said.

"I haven't seen much of you since Red's funeral. I've left you several messages about the reception for the backers of your expedition. It'll be at the museum, to honor your grandfather's contributions to it, and to entice the public about the new exhibit we'll have, centered around Red Collier."

"An exhibit? When did you decide this?"

"The president and I thought this would be a wonderful opportunity. You know your grandfather's reputation in the field. I asked the receptionist to alert me if you turned up here. I just need your okay on the exhibit, and its opening next month—right before you leave on your expedition to the Amazon." John shifted through the stack he held and produced a sheet.

"Sorry. I've been busy and haven't checked my messages." Zach took the paper the curator gave him.

John fumbled in his front pocket and withdrew a pen. As he presented it to Zach, he smiled. "The exhibit is going to be so nice when I finish with it. I'm still going through the boxes you brought to the museum. The grand opening will be a big celebration. Red liked a good party."

"Yeah, Granddad was always the first to arrive and the last to leave." Zach read the sheet, then scribbled his name at the bottom before giving it back to John. "It was nice seeing you. Let me know when you plan to open the exhibit."

"Will do. I'm hoping Friday night in four weeks. You leave the following Monday."

"I know how much my grandfather meant to you, and I appreciate the tribute. I'll be there." Zach shifted closer to Maggie and placed his hand at the small of her back again.

John's thin lips lifted in a bright smile. "A third of the items at the museum he acquired in some way. A tribute is the least the college can do, and long overdue."

The curator's glowing words underscored the sense of guilt in Maggie. She could imagine Gramps's anger over the fact she was working with the enemy. Because of Red, her grandfather had given up his academic career and become a rancher.

"If anything comes up in the next few weeks, or concerning the reception in a couple of days, call Ray. He can take care of any problems or get in touch with me."

"Are you going to be away or something?"

Zach shook his head. "Just very busy. You know how it is with planning an expedition."

A sadness entered the man's eyes. "No, I never did fieldwork like you and your grandfather. Sometimes I wish I had. I'll see you at the reception."

They said their goodbyes and crossed the science-building lobby. While Zach held the door for her to exit, goose bumps shot through her. She peered back at John and glimpsed the intensity in his gaze, directed at her, and felt his judgment. It was obvious Red had confided in him about what had occurred between Red and Jake all those years ago, and Red's side of the story had been different from Gramps's.

"So I see your grandfather told everyone his side of what happened." Maggie strode toward the rental car, aware of Zach's strained presence beside her.

"My granddad helped John get his start, and when the curator's job needed to be filled, he proposed John for the position. Through the years there have been a number of people my grandfather helped. Remember, Maggie, there are two sides to every story."

Maggie yanked open the Jeep's passenger door. She started to say something, then realized she didn't want to talk in the middle of the parking lot with no telling who was watching. She slid in and waited for Zach to climb in behind the wheel and switch on the engine. "So John Kingston knew about the break-in. Who else?"

"A lot of people. I reported it to the police. John and Ray were with me when I went to the house after the funeral. I was donating some of Granddad's personal items to the museum. John couldn't believe what he saw. Some valuable pieces were destroyed. The man cried."

Maggie remembered the pottery shards crunching under her feet as she had walked into Gramps's living room, and her brief anger dissolved. They had shared a similar loss. She would have to focus on that instead of the past if she was going to make this work.

"Actually, I'm glad you met John," Zach said. "When we find the codices, I would like to donate them to the college museum in our grandfathers' names." He slid a glance toward her as he steered the Jeep into the flow of traffic. "What do you think?"

"That's fine." She stared at the side mirror, trying to see if anyone was following them. The sense of being watched still cloaked her. But no cars pulled out behind them.

Twenty minutes later Zach parked in a space next to

the rehabilitation center. On the ride he hadn't said a word and his expression became more closed and dark the nearer they came to the place where his grandfather had died.

He wrenched the Jeep door open. "Let's get this over with."

On the sidewalk leading to the one-story building, Maggie impulsively grabbed his hand as they walked to the entrance. He peered down at their fingers linked together, then up into her face. "I'll be all right."

"This has got to be tough. It's okay to admit it. I know how much your grandfather meant to you."

"Because you felt the same way about yours." Zach paused a few feet from the entrance. "I hated coming to this place when he was alive. I couldn't wait until the doctors released him to come home. The day before he died they felt Granddad would be able to leave by the end of the week. I was making preparations for him to stay with me. Then he died."

The pain in his voice strengthened her connection to Zach. She knew exactly how he felt. Her past was screaming for her not to trust Zach Collier, but her heart was telling her to let go of her distrust. "Losing a loved one is never easy. We've both had our share of deaths in our lives."

One corner of his mouth lifted in a half grin. "Maybe that's why we get along so well."

She chuckled. "We do?"

"I see this as the beginning of a beautiful friendship." He drew in a deep breath. "Let's go. I don't like standing around outside too long."

As she entered the center, Maggie peered back. Again the hairs on her nape tingled. How much was her imagination overreacting? She'd kept a watch on the cars behind them the whole way here, and hadn't seen anything strange. But then, she wasn't an expert on how to tell if someone was tailing her.

Zach headed for the reception desk. "Hi, Cassie. I'm glad you're on duty today."

"Dr. Collier, I didn't expect to see you again. Is something wrong?" The young woman patted her hair as though to make sure it was in place.

"I know you don't keep a formal record of who visits the patients, but people usually check in with you first. I was hoping you would remember some of the ones who came to visit Granddad."

Her eyes fixed on Zach, Cassie leaned forward. "Your grandfather was very popular."

"Do you remember any names? Anyone in particular?"

Deep in thought, the young woman tapped her finger against her chin. "That nice Dr. Kingston came several times. And your friend, Ray Parker." She scrunched her mouth and stared off to the side. "Also a beautiful young lady with long blond hair, and a short, bald guy." She snapped her fingers. "Oh, and I remember Dr. Lanier came once a week."

"Anyone else?"

"There were probably others when I wasn't on duty. I can ask around and see if anyone remembers anyone else."

"If you can think of the lady's or the bald guy's names,

or, for that matter, any other visitors, please give me a call." Zach wrote a number down on a piece of paper. "This is my cell. Just leave a message. I can get back to you."

Cassie's eyes gleamed. "I'll let you know what I find out. Oh, this is just like in the movies. I feel like a detective."

As they left the building, Zach frowned. "I knew Granddad was popular. I have a feeling she'll come up with some more people. Hopefully she'll get some names for us, too."

"Anyone jump out at you?"

"Not really. Except, I don't know of anyone who is short and bald who was close to Granddad."

"Your friend, Ray, was close to Red?"

Zach stopped on his side of the Jeep and looked over its top at her. "Actually, he was. This past year they had grown closer through Ray's association with me."

"How sure of him are you?"

"I'm sure it's not—" Zach dropped his gaze for a long moment, then reestablished eye contact. "I don't think it's Ray, but after last year, I suppose I'm not the best judge. My business partner, whom I had trusted, tried to have me killed."

"We all make mistakes. Trust someone we shouldn't. People let us down." Maggie opened her door and slid into the Jeep. Her mistake had been Brad Wentworth. She had trusted him, and he had used her.

Zach started the engine and backed out of the parking space. "Not the Lord."

"I used to think that. I'm not so sure now."

"God kept me sane while I was in the jungle last year. God sent my sister, Kate, to find me when everyone else had given up. God has held me together through tragedies."

His words produced a longing in her to feel the same way, but doubts, fueled by her sorrow, still plagued her. "We'll need to go by my office before we go to the bank," she said, needing to change the subject.

"That won't be safe."

"But it's necessary. The safety-deposit-box key is hidden in my office."

He turned onto the highway. "Why?"

"Because there was no way I was going to bring it with me when I came to see you after taking the diary to the bank."

Silence ruled on the drive to Santa Fe. Again Maggie found herself twisting around to keep an eye on the traffic behind them. Nothing seemed wrong, and yet she couldn't shake the feeling of impending doom that had gripped her ever since they had entered the outskirts of Albuquerque earlier today.

When they reached Santa Fe, Zach broke the charged quiet with, "Where's your office?"

She looked toward him as she told him the address.

His knuckles whitened as his grip on the steering wheel tightened. "I don't like this. Is there a back way in?"

"We could park a couple of blocks away and use the alley behind the building."

With each mile they drew closer to her office, the tension mounted, until she found herself clutching the handle of the door in her own death grip.

Zach parked the Jeep where she indicated, where it would be hidden behind a store. "You stay here while I scout this out," he said.

"No, I'm coming with you." She pushed her door open and started to get out.

He clasped her arm and stopped her. "There's no use both of us getting caught if someone is watching your office. If I don't return in fifteen minutes, leave and get as far away as you can. Go back to the reservation and have Hawke help you. He's a good man. One you can trust."

The very thought that there might be someone watching her office and that Zach could be captured unnerved her. But remaining alone in the Jeep unnerved her even more. "I'm coming with you." She shook off his grasp and slid from the vehicle.

Over the top of the Jeep, Zach stabbed her with a narrowed gaze. "If I tell you to run, don't hesitate."

She nodded, realizing he was more adsept in this type of situation than she. Following slightly behind him, she could feel each pulsating beat of her heart course through her body with a rapidity that made her light-headed. The nearer she came to her office, the faster her heart hammered. Sweat beaded on her upper lip, and she swiped it away. By the time she reached the back door, she was panting as though she had run a marathon at high altitude. She wasn't cut out for this cloak-and-dagger stuff.

When Maggie stepped into the back storage room of her office building—the only source of light a small, high window to the side—the sound of excited, agitated voices coming from the front greeted her. Her fear sharpened, cutting through her. Something was terribly wrong.

She remembered the sinister presence of the man in her house, and she nearly collapsed. Gripping a nearby table, she steadied herself. *Please let no one else be hurt.* She started forward.

Again Zach halted her progress. "Wait. Let me check it out."

Not giving her a chance to say anything, he moved past her, his footfalls light, soundless on the tile floor. He opened the door a crack and peered out into the hallway. He squeezed through the opening and disappeared for a moment. Maggie scanned the dimly lit room and noticed the few boxes stored in the corner were ripped open, the items littered about the floor.

Oh, no! She headed for the door when Zach stepped back inside, his features arranged in a fierce expression.

"It's safe. The police are here."

"The police!" Maggie shot past him. Her fear had come true. The people she worked with had been placed in danger because of her.

Please, Lord, don't let anyone be hurt. The brief prayer that came to mind felt right to Maggie, as though the Lord was reaching out to her to comfort and soothe her fear.

She rushed into the hallway of her office complex and saw her nurse going into the first examination room at the end of the corridor. "Carol, what happened?"

The middle-aged woman halted and spun around, anger lining her usually pleasant features. She hurried to Maggie. "I tried calling you at home and left several

messages with your service. Someone broke in last
night and ransacked the place. The police think the person
was looking for drugs. You should see your office.
It got hit the worst." Her friend paused in her explanation
and studied Maggie. "What's going on? Why is Dr.
Masterson covering for you for the next few days? Are
you all right?"

"Was anyone hurt?" Maggie didn't want to have to
explain to her nurse why she had called her partner to
cover for her. The less people knew, the better for them.

"No. As I said, it was sometime during the night, so
no one was here. But we had to call all the patients and
make other arrangements. It'll take a few days to get
the place back in order."

Zach's hand at the small of her back reminded Maggie
of his presence behind her. "Carol, this is Dr. Zach
Collier. I wish I could tell you what's going on, but I
can't. And I can't stay. I only came by to get something
from the office."

"You're in trouble."

Carol's words, not in the form of a question, caused
Maggie to glance at Zach. She'd had no experience in
secrets or sabotage.

Zach stepped forward. "With her grandfather's
death, there are some things that Maggie needs to see
to concerning his estate that may take a few days."

"Good. I was worried about you when you told me
you weren't going to take any time off to deal with
your loss." Carol looked from Zach to Maggie. "We can
take care of this." She waved her arm about to indicate
the place.

Through the open door into one of the examination rooms, Maggie saw the chaos that had become so much a part of her life of late. "I didn't realize how much Gramps's death would affect me. I thought working through my loss was the best way to go." She took her friend's hand. "I know I'm asking a lot of you and the others. I appreciate you handling this for me. Where's Dr. Masterson?" She peered at Zach. "He's my partner."

"He had an emergency at the hospital."

Maggie hugged Carol. "I wouldn't ask this of you if it wasn't important. Please don't say anything about me being here. I'm going to my office to get something, then I have to leave." *Before anyone gets hurt,* she silently added, hoping her friend didn't pursue the subject of what was going on.

Her nurse smiled. "You can count on me. I'll keep everyone in the front while you get what you need." She enveloped Maggie in another hug. "Please take care of yourself. Call and tell me you're okay, if you can."

Tears smarted Maggie's eyes as she pulled away. "I will. And thanks for handling this. Are the police still here?"

"No, they just left."

As Carol went toward the front, Maggie headed for her office, down another short hall. She kept her gaze trained forward, intent on getting the key, if it was still there, and escaping before anyone got hurt because she was here. At her door, her hand trembled as she reached to turn the knob.

She and Zach paused just inside. After what had happened in the past few days, she should be used to the destruction she saw before her; she wasn't. Whoever had trashed the office left no hiding place unturned, determined to retrieve the journal at all costs. She would be a fool not to be scared, not to worry if she and Zach would even be able to make it back to Zach's cousin's house alive.

She picked her way across the room to her desk and stared down at the disarray. "Will my life ever be normal again? They've ransacked everything I own. There's nothing left for them to destroy."

Zach came to her and turned her toward him. "Yes, there is. You."

A tear slipped from her eye and rolled down her cheek. He drew her against him. "Please let it out. You can't keep everything bottled up inside you. Something will give, and I don't want it to be you."

Everything came crashing down on her. Before she had met Zach Collier, her life had been normal, on track with her plans for the future. Now she wasn't even sure she had a future. She strained away from him, but his arms were still around her loosely. "Why should you care? Ah, yes, it wouldn't do for your *partner* to break down in the middle of all this mess."

He seized her face between his hands, his slate-gray eyes intense, penetrating. "I care, Maggie. We are in this together."

Tears clogged her throat, making it difficult to respond. She just wasn't sure she could totally let go of the past and trust Zach completely.

"Too much has happened for you to put your feelings on hold. Let go. Let me help," Zach said.

She wanted to fight the sorrow that pooled in her eyes, to stop the fissure forming in the wall about her emotions. She couldn't—not anymore. Tears cascaded down her cheeks. There was no way she could silence the feelings snarling her insides like twisted vines. The pain of her losses, tangled with the fear for her survival, overpowered her. She allowed Zach's arms to encircle her against him.

She cried for Gramps.

She cried for herself.

She cried for Zach.

When there were no more tears to shed, she silently relished the feel of his arms about her, his outdoorsy scent, which was growing so familiar to her. A serenity born from a deep emotional release slowly began to unfurl and spread throughout her. She hadn't cried this much in years—not since her mother's death.

When she stepped back, using both hands to wipe her face dry, Maggie offered Zach a tentative, shaky smile. "Thanks, I needed that."

One corner of his mouth cocked up in a grin. "You're welcome."

The warmth in his expression caused her to momentarily forget her destroyed office. Under normal circumstances they would never have met, and if they had, she would have stayed away from him because of who he was. And when this was over, they would go their separate ways, his life a series of adventures, hers here in Santa Fe with her practice. There was no common ground, no room for mixing. But for the time being she was thankful he cared. It made Gramps's death a little less painful.

Finally she surveyed her office. "I guess I don't have time to straighten up."

"Nope, not if you value your skin."

She grinned. "I didn't think so. Let's hope they didn't find the key, or if they did, they didn't know its importance." She picked her way to the bookcase, with her medical journals strewn about the floor near it. "You and I think alike." She threw him a glance over her shoulder. "Scary, isn't it?"

He chuckled.

She searched the pile of books until she found a large volume on respiratory illnesses, and she hefted it. Back at her desk, she scanned the mess until she found her letter opener. She inserted it between the binding that held the pages together. She prodded until a key slipped out the other end and dropped onto some papers.

"Clever," Zach said.

"I do have my moments." Maggie pocketed the key and started for the door.

As she neared the intersection of the two hallways, she heard Carol's raised voice in the doorway to the reception area, and came to a stop.

"Dr. Somers isn't here."

"But I had an appointment with her this morning."

"As you can see, we had a bit of a problem here last night. We tried to reach all her patients to reschedule their appointments. I thought we had. Who are you?"

The man's voice sounded familiar. Maggie peeked

around the corner toward the entrance, where Carol stood with a man. Maggie's gaze riveted to the "patient's" blue eyes.

It was *him*.

SEVEN

"**W**here is she? When will she be back?" The familiar voice of her assailant rose.

"Sir, I'm sorry, she can't see you today. If you just tell me your name, I can refer you to another doctor."

Maggie heard Carol's strained patience. She sensed the tension emanating off Zach right behind her. His hands settled on her shoulders as though to convey his support.

"I want to see Dr. Somers. My friend said she was the one I should see."

"Sir, I'll write another doctor's name down. She won't be available for a while."

The volume of her nurse's voice lowered as Carol moved away from the entrance into the hallway. Maggie took a chance and peered around the corner again.

"Who's that?" Zach whispered in her ear.

"The man who attacked me last night."

Zach stiffened. He wanted to do something foolish, like charge into the reception area and strangle the man.

But he couldn't. No one else needed to get hurt because of the codices, and there was an office full of workers here. "We'd better get out of here. Now."

He moved in front of Maggie and checked out the corridor that led to the back entrance. Grasping Maggie's elbow, he set a quick pace toward the exit, glancing over his shoulder every few seconds. He cracked the door open and peered out into the alley, stress accentuating his movements.

"It looks okay," he said, but he knew how deceptive that could be. A tight ache formed in his gut as he jogged down the alley toward their vehicle. Any second, he half expected a bullet in his back. The skin along his spine crawled. The hairs at his nape stood up.

Once in the green Jeep with Maggie, Zach quickly started the engine and pulled out into traffic while continuously scanning the cars around him. "You know, this could become a regular habit for us."

"What?"

"Leaving without saying goodbye. I guess we need to work on our manners," Zach said, trying to inject some humor into their dire situation.

"Yeah, if we make it out of this in one piece."

Zach darted a look toward Maggie. "We will. That's a promise, and I'm a man who keeps his promises."

He maneuvered the car around the block, checking out the area—especially in front of her office—before he pulled into a parking space at the side of the bank. They would prevail; they had to.

"I'm calling Carol to see if the man is still there." Maggie retrieved her cell from her purse and punched in some numbers. When her nurse came on the phone, Maggie asked, "Is he still there? That man who demanded to see me?"

A frown marred Maggie's beautiful features as she listened to Carol. Zach still had the strong urge to go back to the doctor's office and confront Maggie's attacker. He pried his hands from the steering wheel and flexed them.

"Can you get away and bring it to us? We're at the bank on the corner." She paused. "Good. Come only if you think it's okay."

When Maggie flipped the cell closed, Zach twisted around and faced her. "She's coming to the bank? Why?"

"We have a security system that tapes different views of the offices. She said he was on the one for the reception area."

"What happened to the system last night? Was the break-in recorded?"

"The police took the tape, which had two men in black ski masks. Not much to go on, I'm afraid. But if I can show them this tape and file a charge against him for breaking and entering my house last night, maybe they can find out who he is."

"Maybe." He pushed his door open. "Let's get the diary and get out of here."

Ten minutes later, with the diary secured in its case, Zach and Maggie left the safety-deposit-box vault. Carol saw them and hurried across the lobby toward them.

The next day Maggie stepped out of Evelyn's house, the screen door banging closed behind her. She welcomed the heat after the strain of the past few hours, working side by side with Zach, trying to decipher a diary written hundreds of years ago by Father Santiago in both Spanish and Latin. Thankfully Zach had a gift for languages.

Before, when her grandfather had read her some of the passages, she had loved the flowery, poetic verses. Now she wished the monk had just come right out and said, "Hey, everyone, this is where the codices are hidden." And for that matter, why wasn't there a big, fat X on the map to indicate exactly where the treasure was concealed? Weren't all treasure maps supposed to be like that?

A tribal-police car came down the dirt road toward her and went around to the back of the house. She would finally get to meet Hawke Lonechief, Zach's cousin, Evelyn's son. His presence reassured her.

Tension throbbed in her temples, striking against them as though an Indian's drum were beating in her head. She placed her coffee mug on the railing and massaged her forehead, but nothing relieved the dull ache. Her eyes slid closed, and she tried to blank her mind of all thoughts, especially ones connected with the codices. She couldn't. Her life—Zach's—depended on them finding the Aztec books before anyone else found them, if they still existed.

At the bank the day before she'd half expected the man after her to be waiting in the safety-deposit-box vault. Only half expected? Who was she kidding? The way things had been going she had fully expected the man to be there.

Despite the heat, Maggie trembled. Cradling her drink in her palms, she took several sips and studied the landscape before her. A large mesa toward the horizon dominated the vista. Its rocks glittered reddish gold in the late morning sun reflecting off their surface. The lush greenery, which indicated a stream, snaked across the flat land that jutted up against the mesa.

The sound of the screen door creaking open drew her attention. With a glance over her shoulder, she noted Zach's frustrated appearance. She gave him a smile that vanished almost instantly because it required an effort to maintain, and all energy had dissipated two hours into studying the map and journal.

He came up behind her. "Under normal circumstances, I would find trying to solve the mystery of the codices interesting, even exciting."

"But not when a death warrant hangs over our heads?"

"Right. That kinda kills the mood." Automatically, his hands, as if accustomed to massaging her all the time, rested on her shoulders and kneaded the tightness beneath them.

She wanted to melt back against him and surrender to the wonderful feelings flowing through her. But the screech of a bird pulled her away from the soothing sensations that for a moment eased her stress. She stepped to the side and turned toward him.

"I'm glad I called Carol this morning to check and see if that man came back again. If anything…" She couldn't finish her sentence. The idea of another person she cared about getting hurt stole her voice.

Zach took her hands and commanded her attention

with his unrelenting expression. "I'm glad he didn't. Is everything okay with your patients? No problems?"

"None. Dr. Masterson owes me. I've covered for him when he has gone on vacation these past few years."

"That sounds like you haven't gone on one."

"Not since I opened my practice. I took a long weekend with Gramps right after I finished my residency." Now she wished it had been a real vacation. She hadn't spent nearly enough time with Gramps since medical school. Regret mingled with her weariness.

"How long ago was that?"

"Three years."

"You're kidding. With the high-pressured job you have, I'm surprised something didn't give."

"My sanity? No, I think this adventure will take care of that."

Zach leaned against the porch railing. "I agree with you and with what your grandfather thought about the references to the earth's secret, its treasure. The place has to be a cave of some sort—but then that was the most likely possibility anyway since the codices have remained hidden for all these years."

"And the Southwest is riddled with a lot of cave systems." Memories she wanted to forget inundated her—gasping for air, fear that immobilized her, dust choking her, helplessness. She squeezed her eyes closed and tried to rid her mind of the images parading across it. But she couldn't. A vision of holding her father as he inhaled his last breath, his legs pinned beneath tons of rock, swamped her with sadness.

"Are you all right?"

When she looked into Zach's concerned expression, she almost told him about her father dying in a cave-in that had left them trapped for twenty-four hours. But that had been such a painful time that she hadn't even talked with Gramps about it. "I'm okay. Sorry, I was just thinking about all those caves." *The dark. The silence. The trapped feeling*.

"It will be like looking for a needle in a haystack."

She *needed* to concentrate on the here and now. "First we must locate the right haystack."

"Father Santiago had hoped to convert the Indians to Christianity with kindness and tolerance. According to the records our grandfathers unearthed, he must have traveled all over what is now New Mexico, Arizona and parts of Texas, spreading the word of Christ. So we know two things. The area we have to look in and what to look for. We have made progress."

"But not quickly enough." Pain continued to pulsate against her temples. She pressed her fingers into the flesh above her eyes. Her mind felt like mush. Not enough sleep. Too much thinking. Too much running for their lives.

"Here, let me see what I can do."

His fingertips replaced hers, the contact electric. Suddenly she was no longer thinking about her headache. Her senses homed in on the feel of his hands on her face, rubbing soothing circles into her temples. She peered up and knew instantly that doing so was a mistake. The smoky glitter in his eyes held her captive. The rest of the world fell away, and all that mattered was Zach and her. The warm spring day wrapped them in a protective cocoon, as though nothing could touch them.

A discreet cough behind Zach parted them.

He spun around to face his cousin. "Hawke. I didn't hear you approach."

Dressed in tan pants and a matching shirt with the tribal-police patch on his sleeve, Hawke grinned, two dimples appearing in his cheeks. "And I made it a point to make some noise."

Zach covered the distance between them and shook his cousin's hand. "I'm glad to see you. I heard you pull around back. What took you so long?"

"I had to feed the animals. I'd hoped to get home yesterday evening, but a case kept me out all night. We keep missing each other."

Although Hawke was as large as Zach, he was leaner, rawboned, with striking features that revealed his Indian heritage. Long black hair tied back with a leather strap framed a face that wouldn't be considered handsome, but definitely interesting, intriguing. His dusty Stetson, tugged low, shadowed his eyes, giving him a shuttered look.

"Maggie, this is my cousin, Hawke Lonechief. This is Maggie Somers."

"Somers?"

"Yes, she's Jake's granddaughter. I'm collaborating with the enemy."

Hawke tilted back his hat to reveal dark brown eyes, almost as black as his hair. "In trouble?"

"Just a bit." Zach told him everything that had happened to him and Maggie over the past four days.

Listening to Zach recite their series of incidents and near misses, Maggie couldn't believe she was unhurt. Gramps had always turned to the Lord when he was having a problem. She'd used to, as well, until lately. Had she been wrong to turn away?

"I'd hate to see what you call a lot." Hawke lounged against the railing with his arms folded across his chest. "What can I do to help?"

"Keep an eye out for anyone unusual at the pueblo. I figure there's not much that happens without your knowledge."

Hawke arched a brow. "You expecting trouble here?"

"I hope not. I covered my tracks well, but it pays to be cautious."

"What does my mom say?"

"She checked her handgun to make sure it was loaded, and said she was prepared. Not much else."

Hawke laughed. "That sounds like her." He pushed away from the railing. "I'd best be going. We are short-handed at the station. I just came home to check on the animals. Nice to meet you, Maggie." Zach's cousin left as quietly as he had appeared.

"Do you really think there's going to be trouble here?" She didn't want anyone to get hurt because of her.

"No. We won't be staying long. By the time someone checks out all my grandmother's relatives, we'll be long gone. This is the safest place for us at the moment. These are Willow's people. Family means everything to them."

Family. With her grandfather's death she didn't have any family left. Again regret blanketed her. Ever since she had decided to become a doctor she had worked long, long hours to get there and do the best job possible. That had been Gramps's way, and she didn't want to let him down. But she had missed out on being with him and that grieved her.

Zach cocked his mouth upward. "Besides, Evelyn and Hawke are very knowledgeable about this area of the country. We may need their expertise. I may know languages, but I don't know the terrain." Running his hand through his hair, he turned to stare at the mesa. "When Evelyn gets back from the store, we'll go over what we think with her and see if she has any ideas."

When Maggie positioned herself next to Zach, her arm brushed against his. Before them stretched a vast area of land, and yet they stood side by side, touching, no space between them. The immense expanse shrank to the small porch, her awareness centered on the man next to her. Her life might depend on Zach Collier. Four days ago she would have been horrified by that prospect. Today she was comforted.

She peered at the mesa, too. The sunlight set the rocks flaming in a myriad of colors. So beautiful. She sighed, knowing they needed to go inside and dig into the journal again for any clues to end this nightmare. But she didn't want to. She wanted to forget for a few more moments that she was running for her life.

She started to turn toward the door when something caught her attention. She squinted, trying to see better in the brightness that bathed the landscape.

"Do you see it?" She pointed toward the top of the nearest mesa.

"What?" He straightened, alert, his gaze sharpening on the area where she indicated.

"It looks like the sun is reflecting off some kind of metal. Do you think someone is spying on the ranch?" She drew herself up tall, struggling to keep her panic at bay. "Could they have found us so soon?"

"I pray not." Zach dug into his front jeans pocket, withdrew his cell and tried to make a call. "We'll have to use the phone inside to call Hawke. No reception out here. I keep forgetting that."

Quickly he crossed the porch to the screen door and stepped to the side to allow Maggie to go into the house first. He snatched up the phone on a table in the living room and punched in some numbers.

"Hawke, there's someone up on the mesa near the house," Zach said after he'd been patched through to his cousin. "I saw something glitter in the sun. I'd check it out, but I don't want to leave the diary and map unprotected."

Maggie peered at the book open on the coffee table. The copy of the map lay next to it, a bunch of lines that meant nothing to her. It didn't even look like a regular map.

"Okay, thanks. Let me know what you find." Zach hung up and faced her. "Hawke's going to check the area out. He isn't too far from the turnoff that leads to the mesa. He'll have to hike to the top."

"Maybe we should leave."

"Let's see what Hawke finds out first."

Maggie gestured toward the journal. "We need to find a way to protect this in case they do find us."

"I agree." Zach began to pace from one end of the small living room to the other, staring at the floor as he walked. Suddenly he halted and whirled around. "I've got it. I should have thought about this earlier. We'll photograph the book with a digital camera. We can put the pictures on a flash drive, then store the diary in its special case in a safety-deposit box."

"I like that, especially since the diary is so fragile. We won't be handling it as much either if we do it that way. But do you think we can read the pages as easily?"

"There's only one way to find out. When Hawke calls back, I'll see if he has a digital camera at the station we can use." Zach made his way toward the kitchen. "In the meantime I'll fix us some sandwiches, and then we need to get back to work. The quicker we discover where the codices are hidden, the quicker this will all be over with."

Her gaze fastened on to the strange map. "I'm having my doubts about whether we can crack this. I've never seen a map like that."

At the door into the kitchen Zach glanced back at the coffee table where the map lay. "I agree. Not even old ones were done like that."

"There's no compass on it, either. Don't most have a reference point?"

"Yeah, that's why I'm not sure this is a map in the traditional sense." Zach turned into the kitchen. "I need some brain food."

Maggie followed him into the room. "Can I help with anything?"

"No, there's not much to fixing a sandwich." He opened the refrigerator and studied its contents. "Turkey okay?"

"Fine." Maggie sank onto the chair at the table. Although it was near noon, weariness weighed down her limbs. "How long do you think it will take Hawke to check the mesa out?"

Zach removed two plates from the cabinet and set them next to the ingredients for the sandwiches. "Since he was near the turnoff, half an hour, probably."

"Unless he runs into trouble." She glanced at her watch and noted the time. Fifteen minutes had already passed.

"Hawke can take care of himself. When I used to visit Granddad in the summers, I spent time out here with Evelyn and Hawke. He taught me to track, to live off the land. It would be hard to get a drop on him, especially because he is going up there prepared for trouble."

Trouble. That was all her life had been the past few days. She would never take dull and normal for granted again. "How do you do it?"

He turned toward her with the two plates in hand. "Do what?"

"Act so nonchalant about all this. People are after us. Someone wants us dead, and you're fixing sandwiches to eat."

He placed the lunch on the table. "Because I've learned you have to keep your strength up if you're going to come out of a difficult situation alive. If I don't eat and rest, I can't think, and thinking is what we have to do if we're going to solve the mystery." He pushed her plate toward her. "So eat. I worked hard to make that sandwich." Although his expression was solemn, the gleam in his eyes teased her.

Maggie stared at the food, her stomach in a knot. She didn't think she could eat, but his words made sense. He should know, since he'd had adventures like this before. While he went back to the refrigerator and extracted a pitcher of tea, she picked up the sandwich and took a small bite. Although it tasted good, she had to force the food down. The second he put the glass of iced tea in front of her, she took a large swallow.

He sat across from her and dug into his lunch. Several minutes later, he fixed her with a stern look. "I don't normally tell people what to do—"

"You don't?"

"Okay, maybe I do. Eat, Maggie. We have a long day ahead of us and you didn't have any breakfast."

Other than Gramps, no one had kept tabs on her in a long time. Part of her resented that Zach was, and part of her appreciated it.

"Here's to another bite." He lifted his sandwich and took one.

Acknowledging the wisdom in his advice, Maggie did likewise, then washed it down with a drink of tea. "Satisfied?"

"Not until you finish the whole thing."

"You are a hard taskmaster."

"I've been accused of that on a number of occasions."

"Somehow that doesn't surprise me."

He lounged back in his chair. "So, since we're going

to be spending some quality time together, tell me about yourself."

She shook her head. "Can't. I've been ordered to eat."

"And you always follow orders?"

"In this case, yes."

"I see. In the future if I want you to do something all I have to do is ask about you."

There was a lot she wanted to know about him, and yet sharing personal information made their partnership more than business. Then she remembered crying on his shoulder, and decided they were definitely past that. "Okay, what would you like to know?"

He leaned forward, his gaze homing in on hers. "What made you become a doctor?"

"I'll answer if you'll answer one of my questions."

"Tit for tat?"

"Exactly."

"You've got yourself a deal."

Maggie took another bite of her turkey sandwich, catching a glimpse of her watch. Twenty-five minutes since Zach had called his cousin. What was taking him so long?

"He'll be okay."

"Who?"

"Hawke." He gave her a reassuring smile. "Is this a delaying tactic?"

She sipped her tea. "No, your question is an easy one. I became a doctor because I wanted to help others." She stopped short of telling him the complete answer. Her desire to become a doctor had been formulated the day she had been trapped with her father in a cave and hadn't been able to help him, to do anything to ease his pain as he slowly died. A lump lodged in her throat, and she had to swallow several times before she could ask, "What made you become a biochemist?"

"To help others," he said instantly.

"And an anthropologist?"

"No fair. That's another question. It's my turn." Dimples appeared in his cheeks, and merriment danced in his eyes. "What's driving you?"

"To succeed?"

"Not exactly. Someone who works all the time and never takes a vacation usually is driven by some motive beyond just the need to be successful."

She lowered her gaze and stared at her half-eaten sandwich. "My grandfather sacrificed a lot for me to go to medical school. It takes a lot of hard work to establish a successful practice."

She wasn't giving him the whole answer. He knew that because she wouldn't look at him. "And?"

Finally she reestablished eye contact, a hint of vulnerability in her gaze. "I think it's time we got back to work." She started to rise.

Her defenses wiped all expression from her face. He reached across the table and grasped her hand. "You haven't finished your lunch. We can afford to take a few more minutes. It's your turn to ask me a question."

"Why do you like to live on the edge?"

"You don't want to know why I wanted to be an anthropologist, too?"

"No."

Releasing her hand, he lounged back. "To tell you the truth, I've never thought of myself as living on the edge."

"From what I gather you've had more than your share of near-death experiences. Just last year in the Amazon you were left for dead, and yet you are ready to go back to the jungle this summer. Why?"

"That's where my work takes me. I have things I want to do, and I'm not going to let fear keep me from doing them."

"Are you a thrill junkie?"

He wagged his finger. "It's my turn. What do you do for fun?"

"Read romances."

He chuckled. "Not have them?"

"It's my turn. Answer my previous question."

"I became an anthropologist because I think the study of humans, especially their cultures, is fascinating."

"I didn't mean that question. Are you a thrill junkie?"

Am I? "You know, I never thought about it. Thrills aren't the reason I do what I do. When my time is up, I will go home to the Lord. Until then I have a job to do, things I want to accomplish." The second he mentioned the Lord's name, a shutter fell over Maggie's features. "Without my faith, there were times I would have given up. My prayers are what sustain me when I'm faced with danger," he said.

"What if God doesn't answer your prayers? Would your faith be so strong?"

"Yes, because there have been times I didn't get what I wanted. Things happen in God's time, not ours. We don't always see the bigger picture. I have to put my trust in the Lord that He knows what is ultimately best for me. What happened to make you doubt Him?"

"I'm all alone in this world. First my father, then my mother and now Gramps are gone. I…" Maggie averted her eyes and stared into the living room.

"I lost my sister, mother and father to a fire when I was in high school. Granted I still have my twin sister, Kate, but their deaths were very hard on me."

"You didn't get angry at God?"

"I'm not going to tell you I didn't question Him. I did. But it was my faith in Him that helped me through the pain of their loss. Without the Lord, I don't know how I would have made it."

Maggie pushed the plate with the partially eaten sandwich toward him. "I can't eat anymore." She shoved her chair back and rose. "I think we should get to work."

The quaver in her voice touched Zach. He wanted to take her into his arms and comfort her, but an unapproachable look entered her eyes.

She headed for the living room. "Better yet, we should go after Hawke. He may be in trouble." She glanced at her watch. "It's been forty minutes since you called him."

"The reason I didn't go check in the first place is that we can't leave the diary unprotected, and we certainly can't take it with us, even in its protective case, as we hike to the top of the mesa."

She whirled around, her arms stiff at her sides. "We have to do something. I won't have someone else in danger because of me."

Her vulnerability shimmered in her eyes. Somehow he knew she wasn't really referring to this situation. "You didn't put anyone in danger. You aren't responsible for this."

She opened her mouth to say something, but snapped it closed when the phone rang.

He hurried to answer it. Although his cousin could take care of himself, he too hoped it was Hawke. "Hello."

"Zach, I'm sorry it took so long, but there's been a bit of trouble up here."

EIGHT

"What kind of trouble, Hawke?" Zach gripped the phone, hearing a breathless quality in his cousin's voice.

"Sorry. I didn't mean to alarm you. It was just teenagers camping out where they weren't supposed to."

"There wasn't anyone else?"

"No, it was perfectly harmless, really. They came down with me. There shouldn't be any more problems."

Zach relaxed the tensed set of his muscles and loosened his grasp on the receiver. "I have another favor to ask. Do you have a digital camera, a laptop and a flash drive I can use? I think it's best we photograph each page of the journal, then put it into a safety-deposit box for safekeeping. All this handling outside its case isn't good for the book."

"Not to mention the risk that it could be stolen."

"Yeah, that, too." Zach caught Maggie's look and smiled.

"I have a camera at the station and can get you a laptop and flash drive to use. Give me an hour," Hawke said.

"Thanks, Hawke. I owe you."

"I'll have Mom bring the camera to you. I'll catch her in town."

Zach hung up the phone, his gaze linked to Maggie's. "Evelyn will bring us what we need in the next hour, then we'll have our work cut out for us."

Ensnared in his visual tethers, Maggie wanted to deny a connection to Zach. She couldn't. He had lost his grandfather as she had. The fact his last name was Collier meant nothing to her in that moment. She took a step toward him. They had gone through so much in a short period of time, and she suspected there was a lot more to come.

He moved toward her, his hand reaching for hers. His fingers laced through hers, and he pulled her close. "It was just some teenagers up on the mesa. We're safe for the time being."

His whispered words flowed over her in mesmerizing waves. For the first time in the past few days, she believed she was safe—in Zach's presence.

He lifted his hand slowly and cradled her face. His gaze never left hers. The force behind his look stole her breath and threatened to steal her heart. His fingers plunged into her tresses until he cupped the back of her neck and drew her toward his mouth. When his lips settled over hers, all energy was siphoned from her, and if he hadn't held her up, she would have sank to the floor.

The blare of the phone jarred the air. Maggie gasped and flew back a few paces. Her hand came up to cover her mouth where his had been only seconds before.

Glaring at the phone, Zach hastened toward it and answered it on the fourth ring. "Yes?"

Maggie turned away, her fingers trembling as they ran over her lips. She hadn't dated much because of school and work, but never in her life had she been so thoroughly kissed. It was one thing to team up with Zach, but totally different to become romantically involved. The guilt she had kept locked away bubbled to the surface and nibbled away at her composure.

"I don't know, Ray, if I can make it."

Maggie glanced over her shoulder at the frown on Zach's face. How had Ray gotten this number?

"Yes. Yes, I'll try. I know the expedition could be in jeopardy if I don't."

When Zach replaced the receiver in its cradle, he stared at it for a moment before releasing a long sigh. "That was Ray calling to remind me about the reception tomorrow night at the college, and to tell me Señor Martinez had to back out of funding our expedition."

"Why?"

"One of his plants in Mexico blew up. There was some kind of explosion, and he'll need all his resources to take care of it."

"What are you going to do?"

Zach combed his hands through his hair. "Ray said that Dr. Lanier and John are looking for someone else to fill in for Señor Martinez. They're inviting a couple of them tomorrow night and especially need me there to sell the expedition to any potential investors."

"Are you going?" She heard the panic in her voice and bit down on her lower lip.

"I need to. Ray not-too-gently reminded me I'm the

one the people will want to talk to since I'm heading the expedition."

"Oh."

A wry grin appeared on his face. "Yeah, oh. If I go, you could stay here with Evelyn and Hawke. You should be all right."

"How important is this expedition to you?"

"Very. I've been working on it for the whole school year. Last year, in the Amazon, I started my research into certain plants whose chemical properties are amazing. I want to continue it now. The potential is great."

"So if you don't show up, the expedition is in trouble?"

Zach shrugged. "Possibly. I had three sources of funding and Señor Martinez was one of them. Now he's pulled out. That leaves a large hole to fill."

"It might not be safe."

"That's an understatement. I know it won't be safe."

She tilted her head to the side. "How?"

"Always prepare for the worst and be thankful if it doesn't occur. That's my motto."

"So if we go, we will be in danger?"

"There's no *we* to it. You don't have to put yourself at risk."

She walked the few feet to him. "We are a team. I would go crazy sitting back here waiting for you to return and wondering if you're all right."

"I'm flattered you care." The corners of his mouth hitched up in a teasing grin.

She huffed. "Don't be. I'm a doctor and trained to care about anyone."

"I deserved that." His smile broadened. "Let me sleep on it. I need to come up with a way to get us there safely, then back here without anyone finding us. I think the reception itself will be fine."

"What would I wear to something like that?"

He chuckled. "You don't think jeans are appropriate?"

"*Reception* sounds pretty fancy to me."

"As you know from John, it's at the museum. The dean of the science department, Dr. Lanier, is hosting it. I'll be expected to give a speech." He leaned toward her ear and whispered, "Which is the real reason I don't want to go. I don't like giving speeches."

The brush of his breath along her nape heightened her awareness of him. "I don't, either."

"Aah, we have something in common besides our grandfathers."

A few days ago she would have denied any commonality between them. Now, though, she saw even more than the distaste in giving a speech. He was passionate about his work, much as she was. And he cared about others. While she treated people who were ill, he was devoting his life to finding cures for those illnesses.

"Evelyn can probably help you with something appropriate to wear if we decide to go."

"Just in case you haven't observed us together, she is several sizes larger than I am."

"I have a lot of female cousins. She's very resourceful."

Maggie needed to put some space between them. With him so near it was becoming difficult to keep her mind focused on what they had to do. "Speaking of resourceful. How did Ray know where to call you? I didn't think you gave this number out."

"Call forwarding. I figured my cell wouldn't work at the ranch so I had my calls forwarded from my home and cell. There are always last-minute details to see to when putting an expedition together, and I'm hoping Cassie calls about the names of the people who visited the center."

"Then it's a good thing you have Ray to help you. Have you been working with him long?"

"Only this year. I didn't know him before I came to the college, but he's been there several years." Zach folded his long body onto the couch in front of the diary, opened to the pages where they had stopped before taking a break. "We'd better get back to work."

"I've been wondering what the significance is of the Bible verses every few pages. Everything is written in Spanish except them. They're in Latin."

"He was a monk. Let's finish translating the Spanish part, then come back to the Latin verses."

"Why did Father Santiago switch to Latin when the rest is in Spanish? Gramps was fluent in Spanish and had no trouble with those passages, but the Latin Bible verses he had to have translated."

Zach sat up straight. "By whom and when?"

"Years ago, and he had several different people do it for him. They never knew why."

"Maybe we should do the verses now, then. We can take them and list them and see if there's any connection or significance, especially to a cave."

"Gramps tried that and couldn't figure anything out. Puzzles weren't his thing."

"My granddad loved them. I got in the habit of doing crossword puzzles every morning while drinking my coffee because of him. Gets my brain going."

"Maybe our grandfathers had the wrong parts of the mystery. Gramps was always great at reading a map."

The sound of a car approaching drew Zach to his feet. He hurried to the window. The strain that gripped him dissolved when he parted the curtains and saw who was coming. "It's Evelyn. Hopefully she has what we need."

While he went through the kitchen and out the back door, Maggie studied the map. A vague familiarity niggled at her mind. Surely she hadn't ever seen this map before, and yet she felt as though she had. Why?

Staring at the black squiggly lines did nothing to spark her memory. Like a mirage, the memory was illusive, just out of her reach. Frustration churned her stomach. Again the question, why was the map familiar? tantalized her. And again she had no answer.

In Evelyn's living room Maggie closed the protective case that held the diary. "Done. I feel so much better with the pages on this flash drive." She held up the device that fit in her palm.

Zach stood and stretched. "And they are clear enough that we can work from the computer instead of handling the book. Ain't modern technology grand?"

"Yep. That's why Gramps didn't work with the diary much, especially in the past fifteen years or so."

"Tomorrow, after we secure the journal in a safety-deposit box, we can get to work cracking the code. The more I think about it, the more I think it has to do with the Bible verses."

Maggie rose and rolled her head to ease the stiffness. "We've been at it for hours and hours, and my body feels every second."

Zach laughed. "Yeah, Evelyn gave up on us." He glanced toward the darkness beyond the window. "I thought Hawke would be home by now. Something must have kept him at the station for the third night in a row."

"He sure is dedicated to his work."

"I think it runs in my family."

"Mine, too."

"Another thing we have in common?"

"I'm afraid so. Scary, isn't it?"

"Our grandfathers wouldn't be too happy."

"I quake thinking what Gramps would do if he were here," she said.

Zach crossed the room and checked to make sure the front door was locked. "We should talk about what happened sixty years ago. We've been tiptoeing around the feud."

"Since we have to work together, I'm not sure it's wise to bring it up."

He approached her. Her body was held in a rigid line. He knew the subject probably wasn't a wise one, but they needed to trust each other completely. The very idea of putting his trust in another scared him after what had happened the year before with his business partner. But the more involved with Maggie he became, the more he felt God's hand in this, not just in helping solve the mystery but because Maggie was hurting. Maybe he would be able to help her find her way back to the Lord. "Ignoring it won't make it go away," he said.

Maggie released a breath through pursed lips and looked to the side. "I know, but you need to understand that my grandfather was the most important person in my life, and just being here makes me feel very guilty, as though I've betrayed him."

He cupped her face. "Don't you see, we haven't betrayed them? We still love them. In fact, what we're doing is a testament to our love. We want to find whoever is responsible for their murders."

She cocked a shaky grin. "I don't think we had a choice."

The warmth beneath his palms seared into him. "We always have a choice. You could have turned over the diary to that man in your house."

"No! Never!" A fierce expression accompanied her fierce-sounding answer.

"You see? You've chosen to fight rather than hide." He brushed his fingers through her curls, and her eyes slid closed for a few seconds.

"I'm still debating the wisdom of that decision. I'm a healer, not a fighter," she finally said.

"Believe it or not, that is how I see myself, but circumstances have forced me to be the latter."

"Like when you were in the Amazon?"

He pulled her toward him, cradling her against him. "Yes."

For a few seconds she held herself up stiffly. Then all of a sudden as if she had made a decision, she sank against his chest and wound her arms around him. "I'm glad, because I certainly will need a crash course in defending myself."

"You did a pretty good job at your house."

She shuddered. "I'd rather not think about that." Another tremor passed down her length.

Zach stroked his hand along her spine, willing his warmth into her. "Then not another word," he whispered against her apple-cinnamon-scented hair. The aroma brought back memories of when his mother had been alive. She had loved to bake, and her specialty had been apple pie. He had told Maggie he had worked his way past the pain of his loss, but memories like this always produced a dull ache in his heart of what he and Kate had missed out on with their parents' and sister's deaths.

When Maggie drew back, he saw her pain reflected in her eyes. As much as they wanted to forget certain things, it wasn't easy. "I know how tired you are. We don't have to discuss our grandfathers tonight. But I do think we should sometime soon."

Her shoulders sagged. "Thanks. All I think I can do is fall into bed. We have a long day ahead of us tomorrow."

"And I need to make a decision about the reception."

She nodded.

He took her hand and tugged her toward the short hallway. "I'll walk you to your room."

She laughed. "I think I can find it, since there are only three bedrooms in this house."

"Still, I would hate to have you get lost."

"I'll have you know I have a great sense of direction."

"Oh, no—another thing we have in common." He forced mock horror into his voice.

When she stopped outside the door to her room, she spun toward him. "I forgot the diary."

He waited while she hurried back to the living room and got the case. He couldn't believe they had left everything on the coffee table. He would love to chalk it up to the fact he was bone tired, but the real reason, if he was truthful with himself, was that Maggie Somers's presence made him forget everything but her.

When she returned, she thrust the computer, flash drive and copy of the map into his hands. "I'll keep this with me. You take those." One corner of her mouth lifted. "I know they're all right in the living room, but I probably wouldn't go to sleep, even as exhausted as I am, without the diary near. Dumb, isn't it?"

He shook his head. "We should separate them. Smart thinking." *Why didn't I think of it?* Her actions reminded him he couldn't let down his guard for a second.

He bent forward and brushed his lips across hers. The natural gesture took him by surprise, and obviously Maggie also, if her widened eyes were any indication. She hugged the case against her.

"The flash drive will be easy to hide. I'll also find somewhere to keep the map in Hawke's bedroom. Good night, Maggie."

She fumbled with the handle, and after opening the

door, backed into the room. Inside she flipped on the overhead light and leaned against the wall. Her legs trembled from the casual kiss Zach had given her in the hallway. Her lips still tingled although the contact had been only a second long.

Oh, Gramps. What is happening to me? I can't be falling in love with him. I won't!

Taking a few minutes to compose herself, she scanned the room for someplace to hide the journal. Finally she decided to shove it under the bed. After doing that, she collapsed onto the mattress, fell back onto the covers and stared at the ceiling. She needed to get up and turn off the light, get undressed, but for the life of her she couldn't find the energy to move from the bed. Instead, she curled onto her side and closed her eyes. She would rest for a moment, then…

The mouth of the cave yawned before her. The gloominess taunted her, beckoning her to enter. She took a step forward, then another. Her whole body shook as the black void swallowed her up. Pitch-dark enveloped her, its chilly claws clutching her with fear. A rumble, followed by a swishing sound, rushed at her. Thrown back against the rocky floor, surprisingly soft beneath her, she tried to breathe in the musky air. She couldn't!

Pinned under something huge, Maggie opened her eyes. A black ski-masked face loomed above her. The sharp blade of a knife pressed into her throat as a familiar odor emanated from her attacker. Garlic.

"If you don't want to die tonight, you'll keep quiet and tell me where the diary is."

The gruff threat froze her. Her mind blanked. All she saw was the man's blue eyes and black mask. Visions of the knife cutting into her flesh filled her thoughts.

Then a sound off to the side caused her to slice her glance in that direction. Another huge man in a ski mask and with hairy arms guarded the door. Paralyzed with fear, as though she really did stand in the middle of a dark cave, Maggie looked back at her attacker, sitting on her chest and making each inhalation difficult and shallow.

"Okay," she mumbled through dry, dry lips.

He eased the pressure of the blade on her neck. "Where is it?"

"Under the bed."

He motioned to the other man to get the diary. The whole time his gaze stayed on her, his cold blue eyes drilling into hers. "Just remember, if you try anything, you'll get hurt, as will your friends."

As his accomplice rose with the case in hand and checked its contents, Maggie caught a glimpse of a gun the man had tucked into his pants.

Her tormentor smiled, turning the knife until the pointed end poked her. He slid it down her neck. "It's good to see you've smartened up."

"C'mon. We need to get out of here," his partner said. "We've got what we came for." He started for the window.

"What do I do about her?" her tormentor asked.

"Kill her."

NINE

The words *kill her* struck terror in Maggie's heart.

Her attacker's icy stare stabbed into her while his beefy hand covered her mouth. The salty taste of his sweat on his skin sickened her.

"Ah, such a shame I'm in a hurry. We could have some fun."

She couldn't take her gaze from his. His contorted image swam in front of her as fear paralyzed her. For a fleeting second a vision of Brad Wentworth swam in front of her eyes. Then the nick of the knife brought her out of her trance. She was going to die.

Lord, help!

"Such a waste." He shifted.

Headlights sliced across the wall. He jerked up and around toward the window, his hand slipping some from her mouth. "What the—"

He moved enough to free one of her arms. She yanked it up, grabbing for anything on the table to use as a weapon, while her scream rocked the room. She **grasped something solid as he cursed and swiveled** back toward her. His grip on the knife tightened. He pulled it back as if to ram it into her heart.

She twisted and screamed again, slamming the alarm clock into the side of his face. His eyes widened. He shook his head. The gleam of the metal caught Maggie's attention, poised above her for that split second before it started its downward trek.

The door crashed open. Zach rushed inside, diverting her attacker enough that she managed to roll away as the point of the steel plunged toward her. The knife stabbed the mattress next to her arm, the blade cutting through her shirt and skin. For a few heartbeats she felt nothing, then pain radiated upward from the wound.

Her attacker pulled the weapon out of the mattress and shot off the bed to face Zach. Heedless of the danger he was in, Zach rushed him as if he were a linebacker. Anger set Zach's face in a feral look.

The masked man lunged toward Zach. Before the steel found its mark, the blast of a gun thundered through the air. Her ears ringing from the sound, Maggie scrambled away while her assailant fell back on the bed, the knife dropping to the floor. He clutched his arm, blood pouring out between his fingers.

Maggie looked toward the doorway, the stench of sulfur in the air. Evelyn pointed a handgun at their assailant while Zach snatched up the knife.

Legs shaking, Maggie stood on the far side of the bed, staring at the scene before her. The man bled all over the covers, his curses echoing through the room.

"Call Hawke, Zach." Evelyn moved forward.

"Here, let me have that, and you go call your son."

Zach slipped the knife into his back pocket, then took the gun. As Evelyn left, his glance flicked over Maggie. "Are you okay?"

"Yeah," she choked out, the smell of gunpowder nauseating.

"Are you sure?" His gaze lit upon her arm, his expression grim as he took in her injury.

She peered down at the trail of blood streaking down her sleeve. She examined the wound, which burned. "Just a scratch."

Zach fastened his gaze on the man who continued to clasp his own arm, groaning. "Who hired you?" Zach demanded.

Maggie's assailant sent Zach a frosty look.

Zach stepped forward. "We've got you cold for attempted murder."

"Another man took the diary." Maggie pointed toward the open window. "He went that way."

Zach swept his glance toward Maggie before settling it on her attacker. The anger in his features intensified. "Who's your partner?"

Her attacker's glare narrowed, his mouth set in a thin line to emphasize he wasn't going to talk.

"Suit yourself. It's your life that will be rotting in prison."

Evelyn appeared in the doorway. "Hawke will be here shortly. He was coming up the road toward the house when an SUV shot out from the side behind him and sped away. He's in pursuit."

"It seems your partner has left you to take the fall." Zach gestured with the .38. "Evelyn, can you see to

Maggie? She's been hurt by this scumbag. I'll keep him company until Hawke returns."

The menacing edge to Zach's voice underscored his fury, while his expression went neutral. Maggie shivered, glad that Zach was on her side in that moment. She sidled toward the door, keeping her eye on her attacker the whole way.

Out in the hall, with Evelyn, the trembling that Maggie had held at bay encompassed her from head to toe. She hugged her arms to her and tried to stop it. She couldn't.

"Child, let's get you fixed up. Then when Hawke takes our prisoner to jail we can go to the clinic in town." Evelyn placed an arm around her to guide her toward the bathroom at the end of the corridor.

The very idea of being around strangers churned her stomach. "No, I can take care of this. It really is only a scratch."

"Thank You, Lord."

"Yes," Maggie whispered, remembering her short prayer for help. It had come in the form of Zach and Evelyn. *Thank You, God. I'm glad You were with me or…* Another shake trembled down her length.

"Come on. Have a seat over there while I get my first-aid kit."

Maggie collapsed onto the cold lip of the tub, trying desperately to keep her emotions in control. If she thought about what had happened in the bedroom, she was afraid she would fall apart. She couldn't afford to. She drew on her experience as a doctor, dealing with emergencies, to keep her composure.

Evelyn cut away Maggie's bloodied sleeve to expose

her hurt arm. "I'm glad it's not too deep," Evelyn said. She began to cleanse the wound.

Zach listened to Maggie and Evelyn moving down the hall toward the bathroom, the whole time drilling his gaze into the intruder. "It looks like your partner abandoned you. There's no honor among thieves. I'd complain to the guy that hired you."

The man shifted on the bed, a moan slipping past his lips. "I need medical help. I'm dying here."

"That's the chance you take when you assault someone so far from town. Help is miles and miles away." Zach swept his gaze to the wound oozing blood. "Good thing for you my cousin is an expert shot. She wanted you alive, or you would be dead right now."

The large man glared at Zach. "I know nothing."

Zach gritted his teeth and tightened his hold on the .38. The urge to pull the trigger needled his conscience. He wanted to so badly. He had a feeling this man and his partner were responsible for both Maggie's grandfather's and his grandfather's deaths. But worse, he *knew* they were behind Maggie's assaults. Patience, something Hawke had taught him, calmed his nerves, and he eased his grip on the weapon. But his full attention remained trained on the attacker.

Silence ensued—a stress-racked silence—as they stared at each other, gauging, assessing.

The man struggled to sit up, his back against the headboard. "I don't know who hired us. That's the truth."

"You'd have me believe you don't know who employed you? Do I look stupid to you?"

Maggie's assailant leaned forward, wincing. "Believe what you want. I'm just the hired help. I work for the highest bidder who contacts me through the Internet."

Zach didn't doubt the man's words. "Who's your partner?"

"You ain't getting that from me. Do I look stupid to you?"

"What's your name?"

The man clamped his lips together, sinking back against the headboard.

Through the front window Zach saw a pair of lights coming toward the house. "Evelyn," he shouted. When his cousin stepped into the doorway, he continued, "I think Hawke has arrived, but I don't want to take anything for granted. Watch him while I make sure it's your son."

Zach looked beyond his cousin to Maggie, her face bleached of color. After giving Evelyn the .38, Zach guided Maggie toward the living room.

He gently pressed her down on the couch. "Sit here. Rest."

"You won't get an argument out of me on that one."

The fact she wasn't resisting his order worried Zach. Her pale features played across his mind as he made his way into the kitchen and out the back door. Hawke pulled to a stop near the stoop and climbed from his Jeep.

As Hawke mounted the steps, he removed his handcuffs. "The SUV got away. Mom said she caught an intruder."

"You won't need those. She shot him in the arm."

"I'm not taking any chances. Backup is on its way. What happened here?" Hawke followed him into the house.

"I'll let Maggie tell you after you secure the man." Zach passed through the living room. His glance immediately sought Maggie to make sure she was all right. Her face still drained of color, she attempted a smile that vanished instantly.

"We'll be back in a sec, Maggie." Hawke made his way to the bedroom. Taking the intruder's good arm, he handcuffed him to the bedpost. "That should keep him still while I talk with Maggie." He turned toward his mother. "You okay?"

"I'm fine. I'll just stay in here with this—" Evelyn waved her .38 toward the assailant "—while you question Maggie and Zach."

Hawke chuckled as he trailed after Zach toward the living room. "Mom's a better shot than I am. That man picked the wrong woman to go up against."

"Not just Evelyn but Maggie, too." *She's a fighter,* Zach realized as he entered the living room.

Hawke sat on the coffee table facing Maggie. "Can you tell me what happened?"

Maggie inhaled several deep breaths, the white bandage around her left arm in stark contrast with the chocolate-brown of the cushion she leaned back on. "I fell asleep. The next thing I knew he had me pinned to the bed with a knife at my throat."

Zach stood behind her, placing a hand on her shoulder.

She glanced back at him and continued. "He wanted to know where the diary was. I told him. The other man took it and left through the window, giving orders to kill me."

Zach felt her quake and lay his other hand on her shoulder. His anger renewed itself and it took a supreme effort for him not to storm down the hall, wrench the gun from Evelyn and finish the man off.

Jesus, that's not Your way, but I'm mighty tempted. Give me the patience I need.

"Thankfully that's when Zach and Evelyn came in."

Hawke pushed to his feet. "I guess I need to have a little word with the prisoner now."

The stern tone in his voice spoke of Hawke's own struggle to remain patient. If anyone could get the partner's name, it would be Hawke.

Another set of headlights flashed through the open curtains and illuminated the far wall. "That will be one of my officers. Show him back, Zach."

Zach did as his cousin instructed and then watched as the officers hauled the assailant away. After that Zach helped Evelyn clean up Maggie's bed, stripping off the covers, which were soaked with blood.

When he glimpsed the red on the mattress, he said, "I'll get you a new one. I'm sorry I brought this to your doorstep. I don't know how they found us so soon."

"That's a good question, one we should try to answer."

"We?"

Evelyn held the bundle of ruined bedding. "Yes, we. We are your family and family helps each other. I'm glad you came here. Otherwise this might not have ended so well."

Zach peered toward the living room where Maggie lay curled on the couch. "I'm not sure it ended so well."

"She's alive. You and I are alive. It did end well. But the best thing that happened is that we have one of the attackers. If there's information to be had, Hawke will get it." She started forward. "You need to take care of your…friend."

The slight pause before the word *friend* made Zach chuckle. "That's all she is, Evelyn, so quit thinking there's more."

His cousin harrumphed. "It seems to me there's more going on between you two than merely friendship. And I know Willow would have been happy to have an end to the feud between the two families." Evelyn walked into the living room and kept going toward the kitchen.

The sound of the back door opening and closing stirred Maggie on the couch. She looked up toward Zach, the dim light on the table across the room casting her ashen features in the shadows.

He came to her side and knelt, brushing her hair from her face. "You okay?"

"No. Give me a few hours to sleep, then I'll be ready to go. We have to solve the mystery before whoever has the diary does. They are not going to get the codices."

"We don't have to go after them now. They think they have all the information, so they should leave us alone."

"They—whoever they are—will not win. They killed our grandfathers. This was important to Gramps and your granddad." She scooted to a sitting position. "Besides, we have a good head start on them. They don't know we have copies of everything. We have the advantage. I think we can solve the code in the diary, get there and retrieve the codices before they know what hit them."

"Are you sure, Maggie? I can do this without you. I don't want to put you in any more danger."

"We're partners. Are you backing out of our deal?"

The anger in her voice blasted him, making him realize she would be formidable if crossed. Again he thought about how much of a fighter she was. "No. It won't be easy. Anytime you want to back out, just say so. I'll understand."

She tilted up her chin. "I'm made of tougher stuff than you think. I'll be all right."

His gaze swept to the nick on her neck. He touched the spot. If anything happened to her, he would never forgive himself, but her ardent tone made it perfectly clear she wouldn't let him proceed without her. He couldn't have her trying to find the codices on her own. The stubborn set of her jaw attested to that possibility. At least if they were together he could protect her.

"He hurt you there, too." He stroked his finger under the small cut.

She covered his hand. "Just a scratch. It doesn't even bother me." She started to rise, swayed and collapsed back onto the couch.

"Yeah, sure, you're okay."

"Not yet, but I will be. That's a promise." Determination marked each word whispered in the quiet. "I just got up too fast."

"Why don't you stay on the couch and try to get some sleep? I can sit over there in that chair and keep an eye on you." He gestured toward a lounger.

She shook her head. "You need your rest as much as I do. Especially if we are going to try and solve this mystery. As a doctor I know about the effects of sleep deprivation. I'll be fine in the bedroom. They have what they want. I can't see the partner coming back tonight."

"You can't go back in that room. The mattress is soaked with blood."

"Then…" She scrunched her mouth into a frown.

"Here, let me help you." He half expected her to protest, but when he put his arm around her and assisted her to stand, she didn't say a word. "You're going to sleep in the bedroom I was using. I'll sleep out here."

She sagged against him as he guided her down the hallway to the last door on the right. "Don't let me sleep past seven. We have a lot of work ahead of us tomorrow."

He went into the bedroom and checked to make sure the window was locked, then came back to the entrance where Maggie still stood. "Just a precaution. I don't think anyone will be bothering us tonight, either." The black circles beneath her eyes knotted his stomach.

She peered toward the bed. "I'm so exhausted I don't think I'll have any trouble sleeping in spite of what happened."

Although she tried to act as if she would be all right,

Zach saw the fear that shadowed her eyes. "I promise you'll be safe tonight," was all he could say.

He hated the feeling of helplessness he'd experienced in the wake of her ordeal. He caressed his finger across her cheek, wishing he could wipe away the evidence of the past few hours. But its mark was evident on her pale skin. No matter how invincible she wanted to appear, she wasn't.

"Good night, and thanks for saving me." She twisted around to enter the bedroom.

He couldn't let her go like that. He halted her with a hand on her shoulder and swung her around toward him. "I can sleep on the floor in the room if that will make you feel safer."

She chuckled. "No, you would be a distraction. But thanks for the offer."

His hands framed her face while his lips whispered across her cheeks where the dark circles were. Then his mouth claimed hers, not in a demanding kiss but in a gentle touch, meant to reassure her.

When he released his hold, she backed away, her fingers grazing across her lips. "I'm supposed to sleep after that? You're not playing fair." Another chuckle peppered the air.

He grinned. "Good night, Maggie."

After closing the door, he listened to her walk to the bed, then he retraced his steps to the living room, where he pulled the coverlet off the couch. He strode back down the hall and stretched out on the floor before the door where Maggie was. He had made a promise he intended to keep. No one was going to hurt her tonight.

* * *

The aroma of coffee awakened Maggie. She opened one eye to sunlight streaming through the slit in the curtains of the bedroom window. Bright sunlight! She bolted up and checked her watch. Nine o'clock!

Quickly she threw back the covers and rose. The sudden movement left her light-headed. She paused, gripping the bedpost. After the room stopped spinning, she carefully made her way to the door. When she opened it, she found Zach lying on the floor in the hallway, wrapped in a comforter, his head cradled on one arm.

His eyes blinked open. He smiled up at her. "Good morning."

"It's nine."

He sat up. "It is?" He looked at his own watch while taking a deep breath of the coffee-scented air. "I guess we all overslept."

Maggie stepped over his stretched-out legs. "We have a lot to do, and we're already two hours behind schedule."

She entered the kitchen with Zach right behind her. At the table Hawke sat with Evelyn, each holding a mug and taking sips. Maggie made a beeline for the pot on the stove and poured herself a cup. After she'd gone to bed last night, she had lain awake for a couple of hours before her mind had shut down enough for sleep to take over. Consequently she felt as if she were walking around in a fog.

"Did you find out anything useful from that man?" Zach asked Hawke as he sat next to Maggie at the table, his own mug full, steam drifting toward the ceiling.

"His name is Joe Bailey, and I think the Albuquerque police have a lead on the man he usually teams up with. They're checking out an address and will call me when they find out anything."

"So there's a chance we'll get the diary back?" Maggie blew on the hot liquid to cool it down. She needed caffeine, lots of it, and fast.

"Maybe, if he hasn't handed it off to whoever hired him."

"According to Bailey, he and his partner didn't know who hired them." Zach sipped his coffee.

"You don't need the diary, do you?" Evelyn rose and walked to the pot to refill her cup.

"No, but it would be nice to be able to donate the journal to the museum, with the codices." Maggie finally took a drink.

"I like your positive thinking," Zach said with a laugh. "We could use some—"

The ringing of the phone cut off his next words. Hawke hurried into the living room to answer it. Maggie strained to listen to what Zach's cousin was saying, but low murmurs were all she heard. When he reentered the kitchen a few minutes later, the look on Hawke's face didn't bode well for them.

"The police found Jeremy Huffman, Bailey's accomplice, murdered in his apartment, and there was no sign of the diary." Hawke eased into his chair and took a gulp of his drink. "Bailey might not know who hired them, but I wonder if Huffman did, and that was the reason he was killed."

Maggie crossed her arms and rubbed her hands up

and down them to warm her chilled body. Whoever wanted the codices didn't care who was murdered in the process.

"Maybe Bailey knows and isn't saying." Zach emptied his mug.

"I'll have another word with him this afternoon. First, I need some sleep." Hawke shoved his chair back and rose. "I'm so tired this coffee isn't phasing me."

"Use my bedroom, son," Evelyn said.

Zach's cousin nodded and left the room while Evelyn went to the refrigerator and opened it. "I'm fixing a big breakfast. We'll need brain power to solve the mystery."

"May I help you?" Maggie asked, and started to stand.

Evelyn waved her down. "No, I've got it taken care of."

While his cousin began preparing the food, Maggie speared Zach with a look, drawing his full attention. "Thank you."

He lifted a brow. "For what?"

"Camping outside my door last night. I went to the bathroom and almost tripped over you. I couldn't sleep, but when I got back to the room and lay down, I went right to bed. I knew nothing else would happen to me." She hadn't realized how much his presence, even on the other side of the door, meant to her until she'd awoken this morning, having gotten six hours of sleep.

"I'm glad I could help."

"Have you decided about the reception yet?"

"Since our two assailants have been taken care of, I

think we'll be safe. I owe it to my team to make sure we have the funding, so yes, I'm going." He waggled his eyebrows. "Want to blow this joint with me?"

"By this evening I'll probably be stark-raving mad and will need to get out. But again, the question is, what am I going to wear?"

"I'll call one of my nieces and come up with something. You don't need to worry about that." Evelyn stirred the egg mixture in the skillet on the stove.

"See? That's taken care of."

She wished her other troubles were that simple to solve. She was beginning to think the mystery of the codices wasn't her biggest problem. No, it was definitely her growing attraction to the man sitting across from her. Their whole situation was surreal. What was going to happen when reality came crashing down on her?

Maggie stared at the map on the coffee table, her eyes burning with fatigue. Something was wrong. She couldn't shake that feeling. The whole day she kept being drawn back to the map, a nagging sensation in the back of her mind she couldn't quite grasp. She was missing an important detail.

"So we agree the cave is tucked away in a mountain range?" Zach rose and stretched, rolling his shoulders.

"Well, let me see." Maggie tapped her chin. "How many mountain ranges are there in the Southwest?"

He groaned. "Don't remind me. As I said yesterday, a needle in a haystack."

She cocked her head to the side. "Or a grain of sand in the Chihuahuan desert."

"That sounds even worse."

"I've got it." Evelyn strolled into the living room, carrying a black dress on a hanger. "This should fit you perfectly." She paused near the coffee table. "Any more leads?"

"A mountain range riddled with caves." Zach shut down the laptop.

"That sounds like a half-dozen places. In our state alone we have the area around Carlsbad Cavern," Evelyn said.

"Yeah, didn't they find the deepest cave system in the United States in the 1980s near Carlsbad?" Zach strode toward the front window.

"Lechuguilla. A group of cavers broke through to the cave in 1986. They're still discovering parts of that cave." Evelyn shifted the dress to the other hand. "Hawke would love to get a chance to explore it, but it's restricted."

"That was only twenty-one years ago." Maggie shook her head. "It seems hard to believe something that big went undiscovered for so long."

"My point. If Lechuguilla was just waiting to be found, so might your cave."

Zach pushed the curtain to the side and peered out the window. "What about the Guadalupe Mountains near Carlsbad?"

"That's a possibility. It still has remote places." Evelyn draped the dress over the back of a chair.

Zach plowed his fingers through his hair. "Even if we narrow down the mountain range, we'll still have a lot of ground to cover. We need more."

"While you two are at the reception, I'll go over

your notes and see if anything sparks an idea. What about the Bible verses?"

Zach faced Evelyn. "That was a dead end. At least we think so. The verses had no common theme. Nothing but misspelled—" He snapped his fingers. "That's it! That's what's been bothering me. In Father Santiago's Spanish part, which is the majority of the diary, he comes across as very educated in his word usage and sentence structure. He has four verses in Latin interspersed throughout. They probably came straight from the Bible he used. So why so many misspelled words? At the time I just thought it was because he wasn't as knowledgeable about Latin. But that may not be the case. Maybe he did it on purpose."

Zach hurried across the room to the laptop and booted it up. "What if he purposefully did it to leave a clue? The legend said only a worthy one would find the treasure."

Maggie scooted down the couch until she sat next to Zach, and peered at the computer. Earlier Zach had listed each verse in order, with the Latin version first then the English one. Now Zach highlighted the words misspelled.

"Refectionis consolata appropinquaret praecidit-quo fugerunt tenebris." Zach scowled. "That doesn't make any sense."

Maggie pointed her finger at the laptop. "What letter was left out of each word?"

"O, L, A, E, G, and *N."*

Evelyn moved behind the couch and looked over Zach's shoulder. "That doesn't make sense, either."

"What if it's a scrambled word? Because Father Santiago was well-educated, I should have figured the misspelling meant something."

Maggie touched Zach's arm. "We've been at this for hours, days, really, with little rest. I think you can cut yourself some slack. Between fighting off assailants and running for our lives we've been kinda busy."

Zach tore off several pieces of paper and handed one to Maggie and one to Evelyn. "Let's each play with the letters and see what we come up with."

While Evelyn sat across from them, Zach bent over his blank sheet and went to work.

Maggie did likewise, but every combination spelled nothing, until she hit upon a word. "I've got one. *Galeon*. Isn't that the Spanish word for *galleon?*"

Zach looked up. "That's got to be it. A ship. He would have probably come to the New World on a galleon. Definitely a word he would be familiar with."

Evelyn rose, her paper in her lap floating to the floor. "There's a mountain in the southeast part of New Mexico that people often thought looked like a ship. It's close to the caverns around Carlsbad."

"That's got to be it!" Zach surged to his feet, bringing Maggie to hers and hugging her. "We've got the haystack at least."

Excitement swept through Maggie. They were one step closer. "Now all we have to do is find the cave."

"That might not be easy. It's rugged terrain." Evelyn picked up the piece of paper on the floor and crushed it into a ball.

"Do you think the map will help us locate the cave

now that we think we know where it is?" Maggie glanced down at the copy on the coffee table. "Maybe it will make more sense when we're there in the mountain."

Evelyn moved toward the dress and picked it up. "I hope so. I'll hang this up in my room for you." She moved down the hallway.

Zach gestured toward the map. "We won't know for sure until we get there. Maybe there's a landmark that will look similar to what's on the map."

"It's mostly squiggly lines." Maggie rose to stretch her cramped muscles.

"There's a circle here and here. Maybe that indicates a pool." He pointed to the marks.

"I don't know. It's so arid there."

"Well, there's only one way to find out. We'll go there. We'll leave tomorrow morning after we get some equipment together. If we have to go into a cave, we need to be prepared. We don't want anything to go wrong."

Foreboding crept over Maggie while sweat broke out on her forehead. Over the course of the past few days, she had denied the possibility she would have to go into a cave again. Secretly she'd hoped they would find that what they were searching for was hidden somewhere else. Now, memory after memory deluged her until she shook. Her breaths came out in short, shallow gasps.

"Maggie, what's wrong?"

Tell him. Words stuck in her throat. Her legs trembling, she collapsed onto the couch and hugged her arms to her chest.

"Maggie, you're worrying me."

Zach's voice sounded from afar. His image blurred before her. In his place was her dad, in pain, trying his best not to frighten her. She felt Zach's arm about her shoulder, then suddenly she was enclosed in his embrace.

"Tell me what's wrong."

Tell him. "My father—died in a—cave-in." The last of the sentence faded to a whisper.

"I'm so sorry. What happened?"

"For fun my dad and I would explore caves. It started when I was ten. I think my father was determined to find the cave. He and Gramps felt the codices were hidden in one somewhere in the Southwest. We went all over the place. It was fun until that day…" Again her throat closed around each word, making it impossible to continue.

"Were you in the cave-in, too?"

She nodded. The sound of rocks crashing, the dust choking off her next breath, the rumble of the earth beneath her feet, pitch-darkness pressing in on her from all sides. She relived those sensations as if she were standing in the middle of the cave right now.

"How did you get out?"

She inhaled gulps of air into her lungs. "Gramps got worried when we didn't come home that night. Rescuers dug me out, but Dad had died hours before that. I thought I was going to die, too. Both our lights went out. It was so dark and cold. And silent for the longest time. When I heard the rescuers, I thought I was going crazy and hearing things."

His arms about her tightened. "Oh, baby, I'm so sorry."

"You know, I prayed. But it was too late for Dad."

"How old were you?"

"Thirteen. I was the one who wanted to go caving that weekend. I loved doing it, and the best part was being able to be with Dad. He worked long hours during the week, so the weekend was our time together. I was just so sure we would finally find the codices. I had gotten caught up in the hunt as much as Gramps and my father. Dad had other plans that he changed so we could go." Guilt assaulted her, as devastating as the attack the night before.

"Do you blame yourself?"

She nodded, unable to speak.

"You did nothing wrong. You liked spending time with your father. That would have meant a lot to him. You two had a special bond that I know your dad must have cherished."

She swallowed several times. "But if I hadn't insisted—"

He placed his finger over her mouth. "Don't go there, Maggie. It doesn't bring your father back. He's with the Lord now and you'll be reunited one day. I can't imagine your dad wanting you to feel that way."

"I survived."

"It was his time, not yours." He cradled her head against his shoulder. "Where was the cave?"

"On the border with Arizona. It wasn't the one. We had reached the end when the cave-in occurred."

He kissed the top of her head. "If we find a cave, you don't need to go in."

She leaned back and looked into his eyes. "I'm not

sure I could. I've been trying not to think about it, but the very idea of going into one scares me to death."

He cupped her face. "Then I'll go in, get the codices and bring them out to you."

He covered her mouth with his as though staking his claim. She returned his kiss despite the churning feelings swirling around inside her. She wanted to feel alive. If only for a few minutes, she needed to forget what had happened all those years ago. In her mind she knew that Zach was right. She wasn't to blame for what had happened. But it was hard to convince her heart of that when she missed her father.

A discreet cough behind them alerted Maggie to Evelyn's presence. Blushing, she moved away from Zach while he busied himself shutting down the laptop again.

"If you're going to make the reception, you two better get ready."

Maggie came to her feet. "Yes," she said, still flustered by the interruption. "This reception is important to your expedition. Is everything laid out in your bedroom, Evelyn?" Maggie passed the older woman and started down the hallway.

"All except the shoes. I left them in the kitchen. I'll bring them to you."

"I'm calling Hawke at the station to see if Bailey said anything this afternoon, then I'll dress," Zach said.

Maggie stopped and turned back, needing to focus on the reception, not what she had revealed to Zach. "What are you going to wear? You didn't bring any clothes, either."

"Hawke has something I can use."

"He would have called if Bailey had talked."

"I know. I've got to do something." He kneaded the cords of his neck. "I feel like we're still missing something here."

"Then it's good that we get out. Maybe things will look better after the reception."

Zach grinned. "You mean, staring at words and lines all day isn't your idea of fun?"

She laughed. "Far from it."

He approached her while Evelyn went into the kitchen. "What is your idea of fun?"

The sparkle in his dark eyes teased her, and her heartbeat kicked up a notch. "I have to admit solving mysteries is usually fun when your life isn't on the line. I like finding out what is ailing a patient and helping him get better. Sometimes it isn't easy to do, and that challenges me. How about you?"

"Believe it or not, a quiet, restful night at home with a good book."

"Ha! This from the man who has traveled the world and had adventure after adventure."

He moved into her personal space. "I didn't set out looking for those adventures. They just sort of fell into my lap."

All she could think about suddenly was the kiss they'd shared a moment before. She breathed in his clean, fresh scent. That was a mistake. Now all she wanted to do was touch him, to share another kiss. She clenched her hands at her sides. "So, just being around you will get me into trouble."

His gaze brightened. "Consider yourself warned."

The appeal in his voice drew her closer to him. His hands grasped her upper arms. He bent his head toward hers, his mouth mere inches from hers. The sound of Evelyn returning from the kitchen stopped Zach from moving any closer.

"Time is a-wasting," Evelyn said as she scurried down the hall.

The knowing twinkle in Evelyn's eyes caused Maggie's cheeks to flame even more. "It shouldn't take me long. I'm a quick dresser." Without looking back at Zach, she hurried after the older woman.

In Evelyn's bedroom Maggie paused and inhaled deeply to calm her rapid heartbeat. What had she been thinking? Even if there wasn't a family feud between the Somers and the Colliers, they were just too different. He was leaving for an expedition into the jungle in less than four weeks. He would be gone for months. That wasn't her life. Hers was in Santa Fe, taking care of her patients. She had spent years working toward that goal.

Evelyn placed the shoes by the dress, which was hanging on a hook on the back of the closet door. "I hope these fit. They are a half-size bigger than what you wear, but I think they'll do." She crossed the room to leave.

"Tell me what Willow was like. Gramps would never talk about her. Once I asked about her and tears filled his eyes. I never did after that."

Evelyn stopped and turned toward her. "She was a good woman who regretted what happened between

Red and Jake. I remember her telling me once when I was a teenager that she had tried to get the two men together. Instead of reconciling, they'd almost killed each other. After that she never mentioned Jake's name to Red."

"But Red is the one who took Willow away from Gramps. Why was he so mad at him?"

"You don't know?"

"What?"

"Red was always a bit shy. He had Jake approach Willow for him. Red and Willow started dating. Then Red went to war. Jake had a medical deferment and stayed back. Red asked him to watch out for Willow. When Red came home at the end of the war, he found Willow and Jake engaged. They tried to remain good friends. They even did things together, Willow included. That's how they discovered the diary and map, on one of their trips into the wilderness."

"Were they looking for them?"

Evelyn nodded. "Jake had been doing some research and had a hunch, but it wasn't until Red narrowed it down that they found the canyon and the cave. They thought they had discovered the whereabouts of the codices at first."

"How did Willow end up with Red?"

Evelyn moved to the bed and eased down onto it. "Jake wanted to take both the diary and map to study them. Red objected. They began shouting at each other. Red's bottled up anger at Jake for moving in on his girl while he was fighting for his country came pouring out of him. Willow ended up siding with Red, saying they should work together. Jake snatched up the diary and tried to get the map. Red wrestled him for it. Finally your grandfather stormed away with only the diary, leaving Willow with Red. They began to talk and before long one thing led to another. She broke off the engagement with Jake and dated Red again."

Maggie sat down next to the older woman. "Maybe, then, we should leave these codices where they are. No good has come from them."

"That's up to you and Zach. You two are not your grandfathers. They were both proud men, according to Willow. Perhaps too proud."

"So if I know the history of something, I might not be doomed to repeat it?"

Evelyn patted her leg. "Exactly, child."

"Gramps was wrong."

"No. It's obvious he loved Willow. She was a beautiful person who was caught between best friends. In the end she decided Red was who she should marry. She never regretted that decision, only the fact that Jake and Red hated each other because of her."

Thinking about the anger her grandfather had carried all those years saddened Maggie. He had loved her grandmother, but Maggie had felt there was a part of him he had held back, that had belonged to Willow. She'd always wondered if he had been truly happy.

"I'd better get ready." Maggie rose and crossed to the closet.

At the door Evelyn said, "Willow would be pleased with your presence here. You have fulfilled her wish."

"Willow might be, but Gramps certainly wouldn't

have been," Maggie muttered, although Evelyn had already left.

Fifteen minutes later, wearing one of Zach's cousins' dress and shoes, Maggie entered the living room to find Zach staring out the window. He slowly turned toward her, his appearance in a dark suit and red tie heart-stopping. Every inch the distinguished professor, he strode toward her with a command that would reassure anyone funding his expedition, his attention totally fixated on her.

He took her hands. "You look beautiful." His glittering gaze roamed down her.

She smiled. "You don't clean up badly, either."

"Ready?"

She slipped her arm through his. "Did Hawke discover anything new?"

"Nope. He laughingly told me he would let me know if he got anything. In other words, quit bothering him every hour."

"You weren't that bad."

Zach quirked a grin and held open the back door for Maggie. "I would just like to have half an hour with Bailey. I'd make him talk."

The threat in Zach's words was clear to Maggie. She settled in the passenger seat of the rented Jeep. The sun glared off the mesa, throwing part of its face into the shadows.

"I hope we aren't running too late."

"I can make up the time once we're on the highway."

"Evelyn told me what happened with Willow, Red and Gramps."

He eyed her. "And?"

"I wish things could have turned out differently. Everyone ended up hurt in one way or another by what happened. I used to think Gramps was the only one hurt, but I don't think that's the case. They were best friends. They lost that and never found the codices." She twisted toward Zach. "I think Willow felt responsible."

"She loved your grandfather, but he wasn't her one true love."

"Do you believe a person has one true love somewhere in the world?"

"Perhaps." He chuckled. "Aren't you the one who reads romance books? Don't you believe that?"

Did she? Her mother had pined for her father after his death, and she believed that was why she had gotten so sick and died, too, not a year after her dad had. If that was what love did to a person, she didn't want any part of it.

"Maggie?" Zach pulled out onto the highway.

"To answer you, I don't know. I've seen such unhappiness because of love."

"And that scares you."

"Wouldn't it you?"

Again his gaze found hers. "Yes. But I also know what it feels like to really love someone."

She straightened, his words taking her by surprise. "You do?"

"I was married for four years. When I met Helen, we knew instantly we were made for each other. She's the reason I went in with my partners and started the pharmaceutical company. I wanted to stay home and be around, not traveling all over the world looking for the next big medicine."

"What happened?"

"A skiing accident. She lost control and hit a tree. She never regained consciousness."

Maggie saw his white-knuckled grip on the steering wheel. "How long ago?"

"Four years. Needless to say, I began traveling more after that."

Are you still in love with Helen? The question demanded an answer, but there was no way she would ask it. She didn't like the implications. Instead she said, "When are you going to stop running?"

"I like to travel."

The defensive tone to his words prompted her to say, "Didn't you tell me you liked staying home and reading a good book?"

He sighed. "I do, and I also like to travel."

"Interesting. Two opposing activities."

"I could always pull out a good book next to the fire in camp and read," he said with a chuckle, easing the tension beginning to build in the Jeep.

Silence fell between them. Maggie stared out the side window at the quickly passing landscape. Flat, stark. A beauty she would always be drawn back to no matter where she was in the world. She loved the land she had grown up in and couldn't imagine being gone from it for long.

An hour later Zach pulled into a parking space next to the museum at the college. "I'm glad the reception is here. I want to show you some of the pieces my grand-father found. He loved being an archaeologist, getting his hands dirty in the dirt. He was at home when he was at a site. Willow usually traveled with him and helped him."

A team. A wistfulness spread through Maggie as she climbed from the Jeep. At least Zach had experienced that with Helen. Whereas she'd been too busy with her career to pursue a relationship that could lead to mar-riage. She didn't regret committing to being a doctor, but what if…

Don't go there, Maggie. Wasted energy.

As they entered the two-story adobe building that housed the museum, a brilliant array of colors streaked the western sky. A coolness laced the light breeze as the sun began its descent. A sensation someone was watch-ing them shimmered through Maggie. She should be getting used to that feeling, but she wasn't. She tossed a glance over her shoulder and saw a couple walking toward them, dressed as though they were attending the reception, too.

Get a grip. The two men are no longer a threat.

She smiled at Zach and followed him across the ex-pansive lobby of wood and glass.

But what about the person who hired them?

TEN

The question of who had hired Bailey and Huffman came unbidden into Maggie's mind, making her halt at the entrance to the main room of the museum, where the reception was set up. Suddenly she felt as though she had a large red bull's-eye on her back. Cold, she tried to dismiss the sensation. This cloak-and-dagger stuff was definitely not for her.

"Okay?" Zach settled his hand at the small of her back.

"I just have to remember that the person who hired Bailey and Huffman has no reason to go after us now. He has the diary and the map. Everything he needs to break the code."

"It may not be that easy for him. We've been staring at them for the past few days and only this afternoon do we think we have a general location. We still don't know where the cave is in the mountain, and for that matter, if it's a cave."

"Our grandfathers worked for years trying to solve the mystery. You're right. Just because we think we figured out the location doesn't mean we're right."

"And our grandfathers didn't have all the information. Each one only had part of the puzzle." Zach waved at Ray across the room.

"When Gramps had the Latin Bible verses translated, the translators never said anything about letters missing, and since my grandfather didn't know Latin, he wouldn't have seen that. So if that is the code in the diary, he would never have found it."

"But I still wonder where the map fits in with everything."

"I can't get the map out of my mind. I keep thinking I know something, but I can't remember what. Maybe when we get to the mountain, the map will come into play."

"Well, tomorrow we'll find out." Zach moved forward. "Let's agree not to think about the codices for the next few hours. A break may be just what we need."

Ray approached, a frown slashing across his features. "I'm so glad you're here. A couple of potential backers are coming, and I'm no good at persuading people to donate funds for a project."

"Señor Martinez is definitely backing out?"

"Yes."

"Is there any chance the other two sponsors will contribute more?"

"No, they both indicated to Dr. Lanier they couldn't, but he invited James Wright and Carlos Santos for the express purpose of you persuading them to contribute. I think Dr. Lanier and John came up with a short list, but only two could come tonight."

Zach glanced at Maggie. "This is the part of the job I don't like. Ray is so much better with the finances."

"Carlos Santos and his wife arrived a few minutes before you. His plane just landed at the airport and he came right here." Ray gestured toward a couple standing in front of a large painting done by a local Indian artist.

"Where's Milton Ferguson and Hector Villa?" Zach peered at Maggie. "They are my two remaining backers."

"Mr. Ferguson is on his way from his hotel, and Mr. Villa is here."

"Good," Zach said with a deep sigh.

"Before you start circulating, Dr. Lanier needs to speak with you." Ray hurried toward an older man with a bad comb-over.

"Who's that?" Maggie indicated the man Ray was now talking to.

"Hector Villa. He lives in the United States, but he grew up in several different countries in South America." Zach guided Maggie toward a tall, medium-built man in the back of the room, talking to a woman with long blond hair, wearing a white business suit. "Dr. Lanier is the head of the science department at the college. When I had my own company, this wasn't a problem. We had a budget for research and development that I enjoyed spending in the hopes of finding a cure for an illness."

"I imagine academia is different."

"Publish or perish." Zach shook Dr. Lanier's hand and then greeted the woman next to him. "It's nice to see you, Kristin. I didn't realize you were back in the country. Dr. Lanier and Dr. Peterson, this is Maggie Somers."

"Dr. Peterson was just filling me in on her project in Sierra Norte and her recent find. Quite exciting."

The attractive woman's smile encompassed her whole face. "Yes, this may be what I've been working toward for years." She turned toward Maggie. "Nice to meet you." Then her gaze swept to Zach. "I've come across some interesting plants in the jungle around my site. The rain forest there is pristine. You should plan an expedition."

"I'll keep that in mind. First, I have to complete the one I've got planned for this summer. I have unfinished business in the Amazon."

"Then I'll leave you all to talk business."

After Kristin Peterson left, Dr. Lanier said, "I saw Ray talking to you. We have two people coming tonight who might invest in the expedition. The most likely is Señor Santos. His foundation supports ways to develop the rain forest. Mr. Wright has been a big supporter of this college in several endeavors."

As Zach discussed the two men with Dr. Lanier, Maggie scanned the room at the people gathering. She saw Kristin say something to Ray and Señor Santos, then stride toward the exit. When the woman had been talking about her work, Maggie had felt a kinship with Kristin. They had the same drive. To the exclusion of a life outside of work, Maggie suspected.

As Kristin slipped out of the reception, a short man with a bald head paused in the entrance and surveyed the crowd. His dark, sharp gaze lit upon Zach, and he headed toward them. The directness of his stare unnerved Maggie. She placed a hand on Zach's arm.

Dr. Lanier glanced over Zach's shoulder and pasted a smile on his face. "Milton, it's good to see you. Come join us."

Zach swung toward one of his benefactors, extending his hand for a shake. "Have you been in town long?"

"Flew in late last night from Los Angeles on my way back to New York. I haven't had a chance to tell you how sorry I was to hear about your grandfather's death. I respected him and enjoyed funding some of his expeditions. He will be missed."

"Thank you."

"So what's this I hear about a problem with Señor Martinez?"

"There was an explosion at one of his plants," Dr. Lanier said.

Maggie leaned toward Zach and whispered, "I'm going to get something to drink, and view some of the exhibits, but I'll make sure to be here for your speech." She backed out of the circle before anyone had a chance to introduce her.

There was something about Milton Ferguson that made her uneasy, even though he said all the appropriate things. Then she remembered that a man with a bald head had visited Red Collier at the rehabilitation center. Could Milton Ferguson be that man? Surveying the room, she noted he wasn't the only one at the reception with no hair. She was probably being ridiculous.

After getting a tall glass of ice water, Maggie positioned herself in front of the large painting that Señor Santos and his wife had been admiring earlier. The bold brushstrokes and sweeping vista of a mountain range took her breath away. The mixture of earth tones with rose, yellow and orange added to the painting's beauty. From the terrain and type of foliage depicted it was obvious the mountains were somewhere in the Southwest, possibly New Mexico—probably very much like the one they would be going to the next day.

Maggie took a sip of her water and tilted her head. There was something familiar about the landscape. As a child she had traveled extensively with her father, exploring caves. Her father had been looking for the codices, as well—anything to get Gramps's attention. There had been a drive behind her father's actions that she glimpsed in Zach, a drive she had been caught up in for a short time as a child. She, too, had wanted to please Gramps and her father.

"Beautiful, isn't it?" a deep, masculine voice with an accent said right behind her.

She turned halfway around and came face-to-face with Señor Santos. "Yes. I've never seen this artist's work before."

"It won't be long before everyone has heard about him. If you want an investment, one of his paintings would be a good one." The man, who had dark eyes and hair and a closely cropped beard, held out his hand for her to shake. "I'm Carlos Santos. I saw you earlier talking with Dr. Collier."

"Yes, we are—" she scrambled for the right word to describe her relationship with Zach "—friends."

Still grasping her hand, he drilled her with an intense look. "Then he is a very lucky man, Miss—"

"I'm Maggie Somers." Flustered by his penetrating gaze, she added, "Dr. Maggie Somers."

"Are you a scientist, too?"

"No, I'm a medical doctor."

"Has Dr. Collier recruited you for his expedition?"

A week ago the very idea would have appalled her, but when Carlos Santos asked her, she actually considered it for a moment before replying, "No, I haven't been camping in years." Not since her father had died in the cave-in. After that she wouldn't even go with Gramps.

"There you are, darling." A beautiful, elegant woman appeared at his side and curled herself against him. "I see you found your way back to this painting." She slid her gaze to Maggie. "I know we will be taking it back to Mexico if my husband has any say in the matter."

"It's for sale?" Maggie examined the area for a sign.

"No, but that won't stop Carlos from getting it." She fluttered her hand in the air. "He's a most determined man when he sets his mind to something."

"My young bride has a way of exaggerating the facts," Señor Santos said with a robust laugh.

"Bride? How long have you two been married?"

"Six months in two days." The woman managed to move herself even closer to her husband.

"Congratulations." Wanting to see some of the other exhibitions, Maggie started to move away. "It was nice meeting you. I've never been here, so I think I'll take a look around."

Carlos disengaged himself from his wife. "Let me show you. I will be the envy of every man here. A beautiful woman on each arm."

Short of being rude, Maggie didn't see any way of getting out of being escorted by Señor Santos and his wife. As they entered a room next to the main one, Maggie glanced back at Zach, who was deep in conversation with Milton Ferguson. Short and bald. She couldn't shake the question: was Milton Ferguson the one who had visited Zach's grandfather at the rehabilitation center?

"Finally a moment alone with you," Zach said behind Maggie.

She whirled around. "You scared me." Scanning the area, she asked, "Where is everyone?"

"Leaving. I think my speech sent them running for the doors." He moved to her side and faced the cabinet of Indian pottery on display.

"It was good. Short and to the point. Did you get the funding you needed?"

"Yes, actually, both Mr. Wright and Señor Santos are donating some money."

"You are persuasive!" she said with a chuckle.

"You seemed deep in thought when I came in."

"I was thinking about that painting out in the main room, the one of the mountain range."

"Of the Guadalupe Mountains? They're near our mountain."

"Yes. When my father explored caves, he would map them as he went. I hadn't thought about them in a long time, but I'd like to go get a box from storage. Something is bothering me. I need to check it out."

"What?"

"I think the map your grandfather had is definitely of a cave. I'm very visual. In fact, I have a photographic memory, and I keep feeling I've seen that map before, or something similar."

Zach faced her, excitement in his features. "You might know where the cave is?"

"I don't know. Probably not, but it's worth taking the time to look." She hadn't been back to the storage unit in years. She'd taken a few items with her to Gramps's, but he'd had limited space. She hadn't been able to get rid of them, yet going through the boxes brought back painful memories.

"Frankly, we don't have bunches of clues as to where the codices are, so I'm game. We need to check it out. Ready to leave?"

"I thought you were going to give me the grand tour."

One eyebrow rose. "You're really interested in what Red found?"

"Yes. My grandfather walked away from his passion. Yours didn't. He continued being an archaeologist. I'm beginning to see that might not have been the best thing for Gramps." She stepped over to a replica of a dig site. "His life, I think, was filled with second best. Ranching wasn't his first love. Sadly my grandmother wasn't, either. I would catch such sadness in his eyes, often after he would try to figure out the diary. I used to think it was because he couldn't solve the mystery. Now I think it was much more than that."

Zach came up behind her and clasped her shoulders. "I'm sorry."

"You have nothing to be sorry about. I don't even know if your grandfather did." A small seed of guilt still plagued her. There was a part of her that couldn't believe she was admitting that to a Collier. That part felt betrayed by her words.

"I wish you could have met Willow. She was an exceptional woman."

She leaned back against him, and his hands kneaded the knotted muscles along her shoulders where all her stress had settled. "That I believe. She had two men madly in love with her. If Evelyn is anything like her, I see why you would say that."

"I have been fortunate to have exceptional women in my life," he whispered, his words washing over her neck in tingling waves.

If she didn't move soon, she would be in over her head. She couldn't afford to lose her perspective. Her life was being threatened. With a supreme effort, she forced herself to take a few steps away from Zach, spinning about to face him. "Show me what Red found."

His gaze bored into her for a long moment. "You and I can't keep ignoring what is happening between us."

She shrugged. "What's happening?"

His mouth pinched into a frown. "You may not want to admit it, but I will. I'm attracted to you."

He threw the challenge down at her feet. She could pick it up and acknowledge what was going on, or she could ignore the reeling sensations in the pit of her stomach. His look dared her to.

She lifted her chin. "Okay, I'm attracted to you, too. But it changes nothing."

"Who has hurt you in the past?"

She moved to the next display, trying to buy time. The intensity in his expression told her he didn't intend to leave until he was satisfied with her answer. "My last year in college I was very serious about a man who had seen me only as a conquest. It wasn't a secret that I was saving myself for marriage. He had a bet with some of his friends that he could change my mind. He couldn't, so he tried to force himself on me. Thankfully I managed to get away before any harm was done to me, but the whole incident has made me very leery." She chanced a sidelong glance at Zach. "Then, after college, I went to medical school and devoted most of my time to becoming a doctor. I didn't have a lot of time for dating." There, she had admitted her limited experiences with men to him.

Zach stepped closer, lifting his hand to move a stray strand of her hair away from her face. "I haven't had tons of experience myself. Yes, I was married once, but besides Helen, I haven't had a lot of time, either, especially with all my traveling."

His softened expression doubled her heartbeat. She swallowed several times to coat her suddenly parched throat. She wanted to say something, but her mind fumbled for something appropriate.

"I was blessed to find Helen and share some of my life with her. I wish that for you, Maggie."

So do I. As well as a family. But she couldn't say that out loud. She'd already exposed her innermost thoughts to a man she had known for less than a week. She'd never done something like that before. But since meeting Zach, there had been many firsts in her life.

"Thank you. One day, hopefully." Her words came out in a hoarse whisper.

"That man didn't know a good thing when he had it." He bent his head toward hers.

Sounds from the main room drifted to Maggie, reminding her they were in the middle of a museum. She forced a shaky smile and stepped up to the nearest glass case with pieces of old pottery inside. "Is this from one of your grandfather's digs?" There was no way she could trust the attraction developing between them. Everything in her life right now was unreal, which made her suspect her feelings were, too.

"The switch is by the door," Maggie said to Zach after she punched in the code to the storage unit, unlocking it.

He flipped the light on, and brightness flooded the small area. Pieces of furniture were piled along three walls, with boxes stacked in front of them. The scent of dust assailed Zach. Moving into the middle of the unit, he glanced back at Maggie still poised by the entrance.

The wash of light over her face accentuated her troubled expression and propelled him back toward her. He took her hands. "When was the last time you came here?"

"Fifteen years ago, right after I graduated from high school. I wanted to share my success with my parents. I was valedictorian of my class and had received a scholarship to college. It seemed fitting to be among my parents' belongings rather than at their grave site. Gramps wanted to come with me. I think he was worried about me. I told him I had to come by myself, that…"

Her voice came to a quavering halt. Zach squeezed her hands and closed the last remaining foot between them. "And you never came back after that?" He wound his arms about her and brought her close.

She shook her head against his chest. "I couldn't. We were such a close family. Even today I miss my parents so much. Gramps filled their void the best way he could, but there were times I needed a woman's opinion, and Mom wasn't around." She leaned away and stared up at him, a small smile on her mouth. "Gramps just never could understand the antics of a teenage girl. He tried, but I think I gave him a few gray hairs."

"You! I can't believe that."

Zach rubbed his hands up and down Maggie's arms, wanting to convey his support, his understanding. He'd been there with his own family. The more time he spent around Maggie the more he was amazed at how similar they were. Scary. Something he hadn't been prepared for. He spent so much time in remote parts of the world. How could he ever develop a relationship with Maggie? Long-distance ones didn't usually work out, and her practice was in Santa Fe. How could he ask her to give up the one thing she had worked most of her life for? He knew he couldn't give up his life's work. He'd learned that while married to Helen. Although he'd loved his wife very much, something had been missing from his life while he'd worked primarily in a lab, not the field.

"I guess I need to get this over with. Standing at

the door isn't going to get the job done." She infused strength into her words as she stepped away from the entrance and walked several feet into the storage unit.

He rotated slowly toward her. "Do you remember which box your dad's maps and papers were in?"

"Even as a fourteen-year-old I was highly organized. I wrote on the top of each box what was in it so I think we'll be able to find them without having to open every one of these boxes."

"You take that side. I'll search over here." He moved to the first stack nearest the door. "Some of this furniture is beautiful."

"Yeah, that's why Gramps wanted to keep it. He wanted me to have it when I grew up. I'd forgotten how beautiful it is. We Somers are actually pack rats—neat ones, but definitely pack rats. It will take me a long time to work my way through Gramps's…"

He caught her gaze. "I still haven't done that with my grandfather's stuff. I managed to pack up some of the items for the museum, but that's all."

Maggie cleared her throat and resumed her quest. "I don't even know what I want to do with Gramps's ranch. I'm not a rancher. I loved growing up on it, but I've grown accustomed to the city life."

"And you feel if you sell it you'll be letting go of a part of your grandfather?" Zach sidled to the next group of boxes.

"Yeah. Is that the way you feel about your granddad's house and possessions?"

He tossed her a grin. "Yes, I guess I'm a pack rat, too. Scary how alike we are."

"This time last week I would have said there was no way a Collier and a Somers were even remotely alike."

He slid the top box back into place and turned toward her. "What's changed since then?"

She held up one finger. "Let me see. You saved my life." Another finger went up. "Not once, but twice. I kinda owe you. Now, that's scary," she said with a laugh. "A Somers indebted to a Collier. Gramps is probably disowning me about now." She shifted her attention back to the box next to her.

Her grandfather sounded as stubborn as his had been. As a young boy he remembered once asking his granddad about the feud. The fierce look that had taken over his grandfather's face had frightened Zach. He'd never seen his granddad so angry. He hadn't asked any more questions after that. All his information concerning the fight between Jake and Red had come first from his grandmother, and later from Evelyn.

"I found it!" Maggie exclaimed.

Zach crossed to her and spied the top of the box. In black letters was written, Office Contents.

Her hand trembled as she pulled the flap up. He covered her hand and asked, "Do you want me to do this?"

"No, I need to." Her eyes held a shimmering gleam. "I feel I've lived too much in the past. That I've let it rule my actions. No more." She flipped the cardboard top to the side and delved into the contents.

Her mouth pinched in a look of concentration, she worked her way through the box. From near the bottom she withdrew a packet of folded pieces of paper. "This is it! Dad's maps of the different caves he explored. I didn't start going with him until I was ten, so some of these caves I haven't been in. But I would pore over their maps as a little girl, imagining myself there."

Zach glanced at the door, which was slightly open, and into the storage compound. The darkness beyond suddenly reminded him of their situation. "Why don't you grab it, and let's examine the packet when we get to Evelyn's?"

Her gaze followed the direction he was looking in. "I think that's a good suggestion." She secured the top flaps back into place and started for the entrance. "I know the bad guy has the diary and map, but I haven't been able to shake the feeling we are still being watched."

"Yeah, me, neither. Here, let me put these in my inside coat pocket."

Maggie handed the packet to Zach, the gesture confirming her trust in him. That awed him.

Father, I know You're with us. Please guide us in the right direction. I want our lives back so we can both move on.

He stepped out into the night, scanning the area, then motioned for Maggie to exit the small building. After pulling the door closed, he quickly headed for the Jeep two parking spaces down. He slipped behind the wheel while Maggie climbed in on the other side. He started to retrieve the packet from his coat to give to her.

She saw his movement and said, "You keep them for now. I think they are safer in your hands."

She couldn't have paid him a higher compliment. He

was awed by the trust she was placing in him. "Let's get back to Evelyn's. I'll feel better when we do."

On the drive Zach kept an eye on the traffic behind them, as did Maggie. After all that had happened to them, they couldn't be too careful. The closer they came to his cousin's, the less stress gripped Zach. *Almost home.* That brought him up short. Home? He hadn't really had one since his childhood house had burned down, as if he had purposely planned his life so he was always on the move. Even that brief few years married to Helen, they had traveled and lived in two different places, the last being Dallas, where he'd started his company with some friends. Every time he'd gotten settled, he'd wanted to pull up roots, even after going to Dallas.

With all that had occurred last year in the jungle, he'd thought his escapades, his roving around the world, were behind him. He'd settled down to teach at the same college his grandfather had. He'd planned only to go on one expedition a year, during the summer months. He'd bought his house in Albuquerque with that in mind. So why didn't it feel more like a home?

"Zach, I think we're being followed. There's a car mimicking everything you do."

He jerked himself from his musings and glanced in the rearview mirror. "The car right behind us?"

"No, two back."

"We're almost at the town near Evelyn's. I'll lose him there."

When Zach swerved off the highway onto the road that led to Mesa Rojo, he held his breath, waiting to see if the vehicle would follow them down the lonely stretch of asphalt. Ten miles of nothingness until the town. Then the sight of the headlights cut across that barren terrain as the car turned off the highway, too.

ELEVEN

Zach accelerated the Jeep. "Get my cell out of my pocket and make a call to Hawke."

Maggie retrieved the phone and noticed a missed call. "Cassie left a message," she said, then punched in the number Zach recited.

"She did? I should have turned my cell on when I left the reception." He took the first curve without letting up on the speed. "I'll call her later and see if she found anything out."

Maggie bumped against the door as the phone rang. Finally Hawke picked up on the fourth ring. "We're on the road into town about..." She glanced toward Zach.

"Six miles out."

"Six miles away. Someone's following us."

"Since Albuquerque?" Hawke's deep voice came through the static.

"I'm not sure." Maggie twisted around to look out the rear window. The car behind them slowed, the glare of its lights fading as the distance between them increased. Then suddenly the vehicle left the road. "Wait. He just turned off."

"That's probably Joe Wolf. He works in Albu-querque and usually comes home about now."

"Oh." She took another peek at the darkness behind the Jeep. "I guess it was a false alarm. We'll be at Evelyn's soon."

"I'll be home later."

Maggie slipped Zach's cell back into his coat pocket. "We know one profession I probably shouldn't try for: spying. I obviously can't tell a tail when I see it."

"It's always better to be on the safe side. You live lon-ger," Zach said.

"Those words don't really reassure me."

With a large cup of coffee in front of her, Maggie sat at the kitchen table with the packet of maps between her and Zach. She hoped this would yield a clue, since Cas-sie had only called to say no one else could remember anyone visiting Red right before he'd died.

One by one Maggie unfolded the maps and studied them, then passed them to Zach. There were a few more left, and nothing had sparked a memory.

"Your father kept detailed notes. Some of these cave systems are complex."

"Dad wasn't an archaeologist, but he had a passion for it, like your granddad. In another time he would have been an explorer. He loved discovering something new." Maggie paused in smoothing out the next map. "I can remember his excitement once when he found a passage that looked like it hadn't been explored. He'd wished he'd been with the group that found Lechuguilla. It's so vast it's going to keep scientists busy for a long time." She peered at the paper before her, a thickness clogging her throat. "He told me that caves and the oceans were our last frontier. I think that's why he got into looking for the codices. He had a mission."

"My mission is to stay alive."

"That's not a bad one." She gave Zach the map in front of her and reached for another one. "I'm all for staying alive." When her gaze lit upon the paper she was unfolding, she instantly knew it was the one she had remembered. "I've got it." She pushed the other maps out of the way and spread this one out between her and Zach. "Doesn't this look similar to parts of your granddad's map?"

He picked up the copy of Father Santiago's and studied it for a moment, then the other one. "In this area, yes. But not this part." He ran his finger along the picture of half the cave.

"What if this is the cave, and Dad didn't go all the way?" Maggie asked.

"Where is this?"

Maggie turned the paper over to read the details her father had noted. "The Guadalupe Mountains. The coordinates are here."

Excitement flashed into Zach's eyes. "This could be our first big break."

"No, our first one was when you figured out the code in the Bible verses. This only confirms we're on the right track."

"If the coordinates turn out to be in the mountain

that looks like a ship, then we are for sure in the right place."

Maggie folded the map and put it with Father Santiago's. "Searching this cave could take a while. It's a good size."

"I think we should start where your father's map ends. That will narrow it down." Zach rose and went to the stove to refill his mug. "Do you want any more?"

Maggie shook her head. "Do you think there's some other clue in the diary to narrow down the place in the cave?"

He stopped pouring his coffee and thought for a moment. "Maybe. But I don't know what."

"What time are we leaving tomorrow morning?"

"Say in six hours. We need some sleep. If I know Evelyn, she'll want to fix us a big breakfast."

Maggie came to her feet. "I'm not sure I'll be able to sleep." She glanced toward the back door. "Where did Hawke get all the caving equipment?"

"Some of it is his, and the rest he borrowed from a friend."

"Do you know what to do with it?"

"I've done a little in the past, but nothing serious. I got a crash course from Hawke earlier, though." Sipping his coffee, he walked back to the table and set the mug on it. "Are you sure you want to do this after what happened with your father?"

"I—I—want to try." She was trying not to think of what was to come.

"I'd feel better if you stayed behind. I didn't even want Hawke coming, though he offered. It's too dangerous."

"That's why I'm going. You shouldn't go it alone."

"But, Maggie—"

She pressed her fingers to his mouth to still his protest. "I'm coming. We're in this together, so you're stuck with me." Her hand dropped to his shoulder.

He grinned. "It's a tough job, but someone's got to do it."

"Funny."

He moved in close, locking his arms about her. "We should celebrate."

"Dr. Collier, we'll celebrate when we find the Aztec treasure." She was having a hard time thinking straight with him so near.

"Dr. Somers, you've got yourself a date." He nuzzled even closer.

The very idea of going out on a real date with Zach sent her heart pounding against her chest. Nothing about their time together had been real. What would it be like?

"If I'm going to be worth anything tomorrow, I'd better head to bed," she said.

"The voice of reason."

"One of us has to be." She stepped out of his embrace, immediately missing the feel of his arms about her.

Maggie headed into the living room, catching sight of the laptop on the coffee table. A thought teased her mind. She came to a stop next to the computer. "When you were reading the Spanish part of the diary, were there any misspelled words?"

"I don't think so. There were so many more pages in Spanish. If there were, only a few. Why?"

"Just an idea I had. I thought he might have hidden something in that part, as well, like a clue to help us in the cave."

Zach slipped down onto the couch and switched on the computer. "Let me take a look. You might as well go to bed."

She sat next to him. "No. It was my suggestion. The least I can do is keep you company while you look."

"One of us should get some sleep."

"And we will, after you check it out."

"Your Spanish is good. You take the right page while I read the left one." He indicated the first entry on the screen, opened like a book. When they were finished reading one entry, Zach scrolled to the next one.

On the fifth one, Maggie pointed at the computer. "There's a missing *O* in this word, I think."

Zach checked it out. "Yes. Okay, that's one."

Fifteen minutes later Zach found another missing *O,* then shortly after that Maggie came up with a missing *P.*

"So far that doesn't spell anything. Hopefully there are more letters." Maggie returned her attention to the screen, even though her eyes burned with fatigue.

"I've got an *L.* That spells *loop* or *pool,* unless there are more letters." Zach jotted it down on a piece of paper on the coffee table.

"Why didn't we catch this before?"

"Because we are so familiar with Spanish. It's like in English, when a word is misspelled we often don't notice because we read it the correct way. I'm not as used to Latin, so it stood out to me after the fourth mistake."

When they'd completed scanning the pages, Maggie leaned back against the cushion, her shoulders and back stiff from holding herself so rigidly.

"I think Father Santiago meant *pool*. A cave is more likely to have one of those," she said.

"Or maybe there's a loop in one of the tunnels." Zach rose and held his hand out to her. "The only way we'll find out is by going there."

She let him pull her to her feet and lead her toward the hallway to the bedrooms. "Sooner than my body wants."

At her door Zach reached around and opened it. "Go to bed, Maggie. We'll know soon enough if we're on the right track."

"We've got to be. I don't want to think of the alternative if we are wrong."

"Praying will help."

"You think?" Would God listen? She'd turned away from Him when she should have turned toward Him. Would He forgive her for doing that?

Zach's gaze seized hers. "Yes, I know it will. We need all the help we can get, and who better than the Lord."

"Good night." She entered the room and closed the door, listening as his footsteps moved away.

She walked to the bed and plopped down on the comforter, her emotions in a tangle. She was so afraid that the Lord wouldn't understand, wouldn't forgive her. Looking up, she caught sight of the stained glass cross on the wall across from her. The soft light reflecting off its surface made the different colors glitter. A sign?

Lord, where do I start?

She inhaled a calming breath and released it slowly through pursed lips.

I need You. I need Your comfort, love, wisdom but mostly Your forgiveness. I shouldn't have gotten angry at You. Please—please forgive me. I—I was just so upset after Gramps died.

Tears welled up inside of her and streamed down her face.

I know Gramps is with You, and one day I will see him and my parents again. Please help me to be strong. Right now I feel so fragile. In Jesus Christ's name. Amen.

"Does this seem familiar to you?" Zach stood in front of a hole in the side of the mountain, hidden from view by a rockslide. "If we hadn't had your father's coordinates, we would have had a hard time finding this entrance."

Maggie took in the area. "I don't remember this place, but Dad went caving a lot without me, especially before I was old enough. When he would come home, he'd tell Mom and me about the place and show us the map he made."

She turned from the blackness and stepped away from the entrance to scan the rough terrain that led up to the mountain. Below them, about a hundred yards, sat the tan SUV that Zach had rented, trading in the Jeep as another precaution against being followed. The car's color blended in with the landscape around it, a reason Zach had insisted on getting that particular one. She wouldn't have thought to switch vehicles or to request a color that matched their surroundings. But then this was his life, not hers.

"Are you ready?"

Maggie gasped at the sudden appearance of Zach, slightly behind her.

"Sorry I scared you." He came to her side.

She smiled. "You caught me lost in thought."

"About going into the cave?"

A sigh quivered past her lips. "No. That, I'm trying to ignore."

"I can go it alone. It's not too big."

"No. No, you shouldn't."

"Then let's eat an early lunch, then go in."

Glad for the reprieve, Maggie went to the backpack she had flung down on the ground, and removed the sandwiches they had brought. She gave one to Zach, then grabbed her canteen for a swig of water. Its coolness relieved some of the dry heat that parched her throat.

Zach settled under an overhang and patted the ground near him. "Come sit. We'll need our energy."

She complied, stretching her legs out in front of her and leaning back against the rock face. "So that's why you bought several candy bars."

"Sure. That, and because I have a sweet tooth."

"At least you're honest about it."

He pinned her with his intense gaze. "I'm always honest, Maggie. Don't ever doubt that."

"Okay, I deserved that. I know now you own that cute little sports car and that you weren't intending to rob my grandfather."

"After what has happened to me, honesty is very important."

She understood that, after Brad's lies and his treatment of her. "I can imagine how hard it was to find out that one of your business partners tried to have you killed, and was selling illegal drugs through your company."

"Money motivates a lot of people."

"Do you think that's what's motivating the person behind our grandfathers' murders?"

"It could be more than that. It would be impossible to sell something like the Aztec codices on the open market, and it wouldn't be easy for just anyone to sell them on the black market. I know there are some people who have hidden collections, but you'd have to have connections, know who these people are."

"So it could be someone who has been dealing illegally? Did Red ever run into someone involved in the black market?" Maggie took a bite of her ham sandwich, then washed it down with a swallow of water.

"Yes. He was responsible for breaking up a large ring that worked out of Mexico. I think at least seven men were sent to prison, four in Mexico and three in this country. They were mostly dealing in Mayan artifacts." Zach chewed his lunch and stared off into space. "His blood pressure shot up when he talked about the smugglers and how they were destroying history when they raided a tomb or site."

"Actually, now that I think about it, I remember Gramps saying something about Red being involved in bringing down a smuggling ring. That was the only time I heard my grandfather say something nice about yours."

Zach chuckled. "They were both passionate in what they did."

"Like we are?"

"Yep, I'm afraid I inherited that from Granddad." He was an all-or-nothing kind of guy. He threw himself wholeheartedly into whatever he was doing. She could relate to that. Another similarity between them she couldn't deny. She was afraid she was falling in love with Zach, and she couldn't see how a relationship with him would work because of their all-or-nothing natures that left little room for compromise.

A sound on the path, like pebbles rolling down the hill, caused Zach to shoot to his feet, his body in a warrior stance. A birdcall pierced the warm air, and Zach's rigid posture relaxed as a grin spread across his features. Maggie stood, hearing the footsteps grow closer, but still not able to see who approached.

"Zach?"

"It's Hawke," he said a few seconds before his cousin appeared around a boulder, out of uniform and dressed as if he was going to join them in the cave.

A broad smile took possession of Hawke's stern expression. "Well, if it isn't my cousin. What are you doing in the middle of nowhere?"

"I should be asking you the same question. I thought I told you I didn't need your help."

"Yep, I do remember those very words, but since when have I listened to you?" Hawke shrugged off his backpack. "I couldn't let you have all the fun."

Maggie noticed a gun holstered to his belt, and she quivered in the heat of the noonday sun. "Has something happened?" She gestured toward the weapon.

"No, but I always come prepared. You never know what you could encounter out here." Hawke looked at Zach. "You brought one, didn't you?"

"Yes. It only takes once for me to learn a lesson." Zach's gaze swung to her. "We were camping one time when I was in college, and had a visitor that wasn't particularly happy I was there. I was glad that Hawke had his rifle. That rattler was six feet long and one angry dude."

"I couldn't have made my point better if I had brought the rattlesnake along myself."

Zach narrowed his look on Hawke. "You didn't, did you?"

Hawke chuckled.

"Seriously, you didn't need to come. I've been taking care of myself for years now."

Hawke's laughter increased. "That's what I told Mom, but she insisted. We're family, and she doesn't want to bury another member anytime soon." He spread his arms wide. "So here I am."

"Well, I for one am glad you're here." Maggie returned to where she'd left her half a sandwich and canteen. "Have you had lunch yet?"

"On the way here. I wanted to catch you before you went into the cave."

"How about dessert?" Zach rummaged around in his backpack until he found three candy bars. He tossed one to Hawke, then gave one to Maggie.

She finished her sandwich, then pocketed the candy bar while Zach enjoyed his with relish. His smile, so full of delight, entranced her. This man had become important to her in such a short time. But how could she trust these emotions? Besides the roller-coaster ride they were on, she had recently lost Gramps, the one person in the world who had meant the most to her. She hadn't even had time to grieve properly.

"Ready?" Zach stuffed his trash into his backpack, then hoisted it onto his back.

Nodding, Maggie followed, then donned a hard hat with a light on it. She avoided looking at the entrance, barely large enough for Zach or Hawke to fit through. Would it narrow more or open up? She felt no excitement about finding out.

"I'll go first, then Maggie. Hawke, you take up the rear. We'll leave a rope trail for insurance."

"Mom said if we aren't home by tomorrow night she'll be sending in the cavalry."

"Who?" Zach walked to the narrow opening.

"Every cousin she can round up."

Maggie laughed. "I can see her leading the charge."

Hawke took his position behind Maggie. "Most definitely. She's like a mother bear protecting her cub."

Her gaze still averted from the entrance, Maggie stepped up behind Zach, a few feet back. Her heart doubled its beat.

Before Zach slipped inside, he twisted around and closed the space between them. He took her hand. "Remember the Lord's words, *I am with you always, until the end of time.* He is with you. I'm with you."

Her throat tight, she gave one nod. She lifted her gaze to his, then slid it toward the entrance. "Let's go."

Zach disappeared into the opening. Maggie inhaled a breath that didn't really fill her lungs. She took another, deeper one and moved forward. Her legs shook. She slowed her pace as the darkness neared. Then with another gulp of the outside air, she walked inside, seeing Zach waiting for her up ahead.

Sweat broke out on her forehead. Zach's expression encouraged her. She focused on him and inched forward. *I can do this.*

But you don't have to.

The thought teased at the edges of her mind. Although she wanted to stop, Hawke was right behind her, so she kept going toward Zach. The passage, only a few feet across, pressed in on her, sending her heartbeat hammering even more. Wet tracks of sweat coursed down her face.

Zach's eyes softened. "Okay?"

No. "Let's keep moving." She was afraid if they stopped she would bolt back toward the sunlight slicing through the darkness, only five or six yards behind her.

"Are you sure?"

"Don't worry about me," she said in the bravest tone she could manage, even though she felt hemmed in by the walls, Zach and Hawke.

Zach snared her gaze. "But I do worry about you."

"I can take care of myself. I've been doing it for years."

He grinned. "Touché. Then promise me that if you need to go back, you'll tell me."

She wanted to shout, "I need to go back now," but she didn't. Instead she said, "I will."

Another turn in the passage and the cave opened up into a small cavern. All natural light vanished, and Maggie switched on the lamp on top of her helmet. She made a slow circle, shining her light on the rock surface. In the middle of the cave stalactites hung from the ceiling, glistening, fragile fingers of minerals. Although beauty abounded, it was hard for her to appreciate it.

Zach studied the map and pointed toward the far wall. "This way."

Following him, Maggie noticed two other passages off the cavern besides the one they were taking. She hoped the map was accurate. Doubts and anxiety taunted her with each step into the stone corridor. She tried not to think of the tons and tons of rock over her, about the cave-in years ago. But she couldn't stop the memories from drenching her in a cold sweat, although the temperature was near seventy degrees with one hundred percent humidity. She trembled, her teeth chattering.

Up ahead the ceiling of the passageway lowered to only five feet. Zach walked bent over, then he got onto his hands and knees when the ceiling's height shrank to a yard.

Maggie came to a halt. Her quaking intensified. Her pulse raced while sweat continued to pour off her.

Hawke stopped behind her. "Zach."

Zach retraced his steps and stood in front of Maggie.

Tears filled her eyes, and his image blurred before her. She saw his mouth move, but the thundering of her heartbeat drowned out his words.

All she could see now was her father crying out in pain as stones tumbled down upon him, pinning him to the floor of the cave. Right after he had pushed her to safety. She'd rushed toward him, and he'd called out for her to get back. Dust billowed around him, swallowing him for a few minutes until the rockslide ceased. When she finally laid eyes on him again, most of his body was covered.

I can't do this.

You don't have to. Go back. Let Zach and Hawke go on.

Zach placed his hands on both sides of her head and thrust his face close, inches from hers.

I'm letting them down.

No, you aren't. You're needed somewhere else.

"Maggie!"

The sound of Zach's voice finally penetrated through the words in her mind. The tension in his hands on her face conveyed his concern. She blinked the tears away.

"I have to go back. I can't go any farther. I thought I could—"

"Shh. I know. That's okay. I'll take you back."

She nearly collapsed against him. She didn't have to go back alone. She wasn't sure she would have made it.

Zach looked over Maggie's shoulder at Hawke. "Go forward. This passageway opens up into another cavern. Stay there until I get back."

As Hawke squeezed by them, he gave Maggie a set of keys. "I have some binoculars in my Jeep. Why don't you get them? The terrain around here is beautiful. If we aren't back by dark, there's camping equipment you can use. I parked close to your SUV, behind a boulder."

The idea of camping overnight by herself almost made her stay, until she glanced at the narrowing passage. She knew being in the wide-open spaces outside the cave was the better choice.

Zach took the lead again, this time holding her hand when possible. The physical contact soothed her raw nerves. She wished she could close her eyes and let him guide her to the entrance, but she knew the danger in that. One wrong step, and she could break a leg on the uneven surface.

Back in the small cavern, Maggie crossed the space quickly behind Zach. Her heartbeat calmed the nearer she came to the sunlight. Its rays beckoned, and she hurried her pace, passing Zach at the end.

Outside, she bent over and sucked in deep breaths, her hands resting on her knees. She couldn't seem to get enough of the sweet, dry air. Zach's hand on her back reminded her she wasn't alone, and she straightened. Legs weak, she immediately sank to the ground.

Zach knelt next to her and enclosed her in his embrace. "It was too much to ask you to go back into a cave after what happened with you and your father. I should have known better."

She gave him a small smile that disappeared almost instantly. "I should have known better. I'm sorry. All I could see was my father trapped under the rocks. I couldn't move them. I couldn't save him. I couldn't even go for help. I thought I was going to die, too."

Words tumbled from her mouth like the rocks had in the slide. She sniffed, swiping her hand across her forehead to keep the sweat from rolling into her eyes and stinging them. "His light had been crushed under the avalanche, along with his backpack, where the spare batteries were. A few hours later mine died, and I was plunged into total darkness. I wanted to die then."

"But you didn't. You hung on because you're a fighter." He removed her helmet and smoothed her damp hair back from her face. Tilting her chin up, he looked long and hard into her eyes. "One I've come to care about. Will you be all right?"

"Yes, you don't need to worry about me." She already felt as if she'd let him down. She didn't want to anymore. The whole ride to the mountain, she'd told herself she could go into the cave and be all right. She'd been wrong. Sometimes the desire to do something wasn't enough. "I'll be here waiting when you and Hawke come back with the codices."

The mesmerizing look he sent her made her want to melt into the ground. He ran his fingers through her hair and leaned down to graze his mouth across hers. In that moment she realized she loved him in spite of her reservations about the wisdom of it.

When he pulled back, he drew her to her feet. He rummaged in his backpack until he found his gun, and he gave it to her. "I want you to have this."

"No, I can't take that. You'll be defenseless."

He chuckled. "Hawke has his, and besides, I don't think there are going to be any wild animals in the cave." She started to push the weapon away when he added, "I won't go back in if you don't take it. I know you're an expert shot. At least, you told me you were at your grandfather's ranch." One corner of his mouth hitched up. "Were you pulling my leg then?"

"No." She cradled the cold metal in her hand. "I am, or let's just say I was. Since becoming a doctor I haven't handled a gun other than when I caught you in Gramps's house."

Zach groaned. "Please don't remind me of that incident. I was thankful Hawke could vouch for me, but he did rib me about it."

"You need to get back inside. The quicker you do, the quicker we can get the treasure and get out of here." She glanced up at the sun directly overhead. "I'll be here waiting when you two come out."

Another brief kiss and Zach disappeared into the cave. Maggie stared at the entrance for a long moment. She'd thought she would feel more upset with herself than she was, but she knew this was for the best. She would have slowed them down, possibly even put them in danger if she'd had a full-blown panic attack.

Pivoting away, she scanned the terrain. From this height she could see the dirt road that led to the mountain. At first glance the area appeared barren, but the desert teemed with life. Rolling land stretched before her with yucca, agaves and cacti, some blooming, and a few juniper trees mixed among the scrub brush.

She put the gun down by her backpack and started to hike to Hawke's Jeep, then she remembered that life in the desert included rattlesnakes. She decided to carry the weapon with her. As she descended the side of the mountain, she took her time, occasionally slipping on the loose rocks in her path.

At Hawke's vehicle she retrieved his camping gear and slung the binoculars around her neck, then began her ascent. By the time she got back to the cave's entrance she had killed almost an hour. Not used to inactivity, she lifted the binoculars to give her something to do.

Below her, in the flatter terrain, she spied a mule deer. She followed its progress as it munched on some plants. That lasted fifteen minutes. She needed to come up with something else to occupy her time.

For a moment her thoughts were centered around the kiss that Zach had given her right before he had gone back into the cave. He certainly knew how to say goodbye to a gal. What in the world was she going to do about her feelings concerning him? In three weeks he was leaving for the summer. Then she remembered what had happened to him the last time he had gone into the Amazon. He'd nearly died.

"Don't think about it," she muttered in the silence.

She made another sweep of the landscape and caught sight of some dust kicking up in the distance. She focused the binoculars on it and realized it was growing nearer. When the SUV came into clear view, fear seeped into her.

She trained the binoculars on the vehicle as it came closer. Then she saw there were two people in the front seat. She adjusted the focus and honed in on the driver. The field glasses slipped from her numb fingers and fell to her chest.

TWELVE

How had Joe Bailey gotten out of jail? Had someone bailed him out, or had he escaped?

How had they found them?

Or had the criminals solved the mystery and come to get the codices without knowing she, Zach and Hawke were here?

Question after question raced through Maggie's mind. She backed toward the entrance of the cave, her fear full-blown now. She scanned the area. She could hide the camping equipment, but there wasn't any way she could hide the two vehicles parked below.

Picking up the weapon from the ground by her backpack, she felt its heavy weight. She had a gun. She could use it, but the very thought turned her heart to ice. She was a healer, not a killer.

She inched toward the boulder that hid the entrance to the cave from the bottom of the mountain. Bailey parked his SUV next to their rented tan one and climbed from it. The other man in the front seat did likewise, while a third one exited the back.

The slamming of the car doors jolted her into action. She needed to warn Zach and Hawke.

She needed to go back into the cave.

No!

Pivoting toward the dark entrance, she fixed her gaze on it. If she hid then went for help, she might not come back in time. She peered over the large rock at the three men. One bent down and drove a knife into the tan SUV's tires while the other two located Hawke's Jeep and disabled it. If she had wanted to go for help, it wasn't possible now unless she could hot-wire Bailey's car, which she didn't know how to do.

Trapped!

With nowhere to go but into the lion's den.

Lord, help! I can't do this without You. I need Your help.

Thoughts of Zach and Hawke, unaware of the three men and vulnerable, propelled her closer to the dark opening of the cave. Her whole body quaked as she bent down and grabbed the straps of her backpack, then slung it over her shoulder. She stuffed the gun into the knapsack's front pocket where she could get it quickly if need be.

Then she took a step toward the entrance.

Then another.

She might have thirty minutes on the three men. Not much time.

She reached out to touch the rock wall just inside the entrance. Definitely not enough time. Especially when she shook so badly she didn't know how she would be able to hold the rope. She couldn't leave it down for the men to follow.

With a fortifying breath she entered the cave. Immediately her heartbeat accelerated and sweat beaded on her forehead. She still trembled with each step.

I can't fall apart. Our lives may hang in the balance. I can do this!

She picked up the rope and started following its path, concentrating on putting one foot in front of the other.

"The Lord is my shepherd." She began reciting Psalm 23. When she reached the part about, *"Yea, though I walk through the valley of the shadow of death,"* a calmness descended. She felt God's presence all around her. By the time she ended with, *"And I will dwell in the house of the Lord for ever,"* His protective shield encased her.

She made it to the first small cavern and wasted no time crossing it to the passage. When she arrived at the narrowing of the stone corridor, the length of rope stopped. Since there was only one way to go, Zach no doubt was only using it when he absolutely needed to. She paused, rubbing her wet hands together to warm them.

I am with you until the end of time.

The verse strengthened her resolve. She would make it through the tunnel because their lives depended on it. She repeated the verse over and over as she crawled forward. Her light shone on her path, and she glimpsed a widening maybe ten feet ahead. She hurried her pace, ignoring the pain in her knees and palms as a piece of sharp rock cut into her. She'd left her knee pads by the camping equipment. She had no time to pamper herself.

At the end of the tunnel she halted and listened for

any sound. In the distance she heard dripping, but otherwise it was utterly quiet. Coming out into another small chamber, she swung around in a slow circle to illuminate the walls while she pulled up the map in her mind and visualized where she needed to go next.

There was a passage off to the left of the tunnel. She turned toward the area and saw a bolt-hole. *Lord, I hope this is the way.*

Before slipping into a narrow tunnel, she checked it out. It appeared to be shorter than the last one. *Thank You, Lord.* She wiggled inside the small opening, imagining that both Zach and Hawke had barely fit.

Good. The men behind her might not be able to fit into this tunnel, she thought, and flattened herself so she could slide forward. Sweat-drenched, she sucked in shallow breaths. Again she recited the verse from Matthew aloud to hear her own voice. The words comforted her, and her breathing evened out.

I can do this. God is with me.

She emerged from the bolt-hole onto a ledge high above a cavern. Inching forward, she peered over the rocks into the inky blackness, so dark that her light didn't fully penetrate it. A dead end?

Before she could decide, a rumble beneath her sent her down flat against the rock as she hugged it for dear life.

A dead end? Zach looked at the pool before him, so clear that it didn't even look like there was water in the bottom of the chamber. "This must be what Father Santiago was referring to in his diary." His light swept the circumference of the room. Rock led down to the edge of the pool. "Where in the world would he hide the Aztec codices? In the water?"

"If so, they are ruined." Hawke came to his side and did his own inspection. "Probably the water table was different when he hid them here."

"So this is all for nothing?"

"It might be."

"I won't accept that. Two men have died because of the codices."

"Probably more than that, if we knew the full history of them."

A noise, as though the earth grumbled its displeasure at their intrusion, rippled through the air. Zach was glad Maggie wasn't in the cave with them. "That doesn't sound good."

"This cave may be unstable. Some are. I noticed some evidence of previous rockslides as we descended. It might not be safe to stay long," Hawke said.

"We've come this far. The rockslides I saw didn't look recent. I want to check this pool out completely. There might be something we're missing." Zach pointed toward the far side. "We can't even see what's over there. We'll need to get closer. The water doesn't look like it would be over our heads."

Hawke waved his arm across his body. "After you, cousin."

Zach took a step into the pool. Then another. Cold water saturated his lower jeans and hiking boots. "If this doesn't yield anything, we need to go back to that last fork in the passageway and go to the right. Both were drawn on the map. I wonder why."

"But this is the one that ends in a pool."

"Maybe he was warning us about the pool."

"A trap?"

"Yes." Zach's footing gave way and he went down into the freezing water.

The way back was blocked by the three men with guns, only thirty minutes behind her at the most. Maggie had to do something, and fast, or she would be trapped on this ledge with nowhere to go. Remembering her attacker's hand over her mouth petrified her. She'd nearly died twice because of him.

But even worse, the cave wasn't stable. What if there was another cave-in? The thought struck terror straight into her heart.

She was caught between two impossible situations—both deadly. *Lord, what do I do?*

The weight of the rope she carried reminded her there might be a rope somewhere on the ledge that led downward. She checked the floor inch by inch. Nothing. No place to tie a rope.

The ticking of minutes in her mind renewed her fear tenfold. *Lord, how do I get out of here?*

The sound of a rock falling echoed in the chamber. Maggie looked toward the direction it came from, and her light sliced across the stone facade a foot from the ledge. A rope hung down into the inky blackness, secured around a rocky protrusion.

She sidled along the wall until she came to the end of the shelf she stood on, and she inspected the distance between her and the rope. Maybe two feet, and there was a foothold right under the boulder the rope was tied to.

She peeked over, her beam of light invading the darkness for several yards. Then nothing. Zach and Hawke had gone down. She would have to also if she was going to warn them.

Lord, I've never been afraid of heights. Help me not to be in this case, too. If Zach can return to the place where he almost died, I can do this.

She glided her foot across the twenty-four inches to the groove in the wall. Before she'd secured herself, screeching filled the air in all directions. Something flew by her, then another one. Bats! Hundreds!

Zach came up splashing, coughing. The sound echoed through the cavern. He regained his footing and, when the water smoothed out, peered into its depths. A hole about three feet across indented the floor of the pool.

He flung off his backpack and handed it, along with his helmet, to Hawke. "This might be something. I'll dive down and check it out."

Zach submerged himself in the cold water and swam to the bottom. He ran his hands over its surface, inspecting it for anything that might lead to where the treasure was. All he felt was stone beneath his fingers.

Zach surfaced. "There's nothing. Let's keep going. I want to see what's over there." He pointed toward the far wall, where darkness dominated.

Hawke gave Zach his knapsack. He waded forward, skirting the hole. As he neared the area, the lamp on his helmet radiated against the wall, accentuating the brown, yellow and red of the rock. He noticed there was still a shadow, long and running from the top of the wall to the water, where it appeared there was a rockslide into the pool.

Zach reached out and grazed his fingertips over the stone surface. "There's an opening here! This could be it!"

Hawke came up behind him. "Can you fit into it?"

Again Zach discarded his backpack and gave it to Hawke. He neared the slit in the rocks and tried to wedge himself through it. "No, and you won't fit, either."

Hawke examined the surface. "But Maggie could."

"No!" Zach objected instantly, thinking about the terror that had gripped her when she'd tried to accompany them earlier. "I won't ask that of her. We'll have to think of something else."

Maggie jerked away from the swarm of bats. One tangled itself against her helmet as if it were caught in the helmet's strap. She loosened it and the bat flew away. Before she could tighten her chin strap again, the air teemed with more bats.

When she ducked down, she accidentally knocked her helmet from her head. It plunged downward into the inky gloom. The sound of it striking the rock floor bombarded through the cavern. All around her darkness prevailed. Although the urge to flail her arms was strong, Maggie held on to the handholds. Thoughts of falling, no telling how far into the pitch-black pit, spurred her to press herself against the wall and not let go.

Another bat ensnared itself in her hair. She swallowed her scream, squeezing her eyes closed as though that would help rid her of the flapping animal. *Lord, please help me!* Finally the mammal managed to disengage itself from her strands and launch itself into the air.

What do I do?

Panic eroded her fragile composure, which she had managed to hold together—barely—because she'd had a light. Now she didn't. She looked down and saw a faint glimmer at the bottom. Her lamp had survived the fall!

I can do this.

When silence ruled in the chamber, Maggie pried one hand from the stone, searched for the rope and gripped it. Inching closer, she felt with her foot for another hold and found an indentation. Then, grasping the line, she began her descent into the blackness.

Memories of the other time she'd spent in the dark in a cave threatened to unravel her newfound strength. "I won't let you win," she said. Although she didn't really know who *you* was, she felt better saying it out loud.

Yea, though I walk through the valley of the shadow of death, I will fear no evil.

In frustration, Zach tried one more time to stuff his body through the opening. When it didn't work, he pounded his fist against the stone.

"It must have been that last candy bar you had."

Zach threw a glare over his shoulder at Hawke. "Funny. We need to go back to the surface and regroup. We have a couple of cousins who would probably fit through there, although it would be wise to check the cave's stability before any more people come down."

"What if it's a dead end?"

Zach shrugged. "It might be, but we have to check it out. We've followed the monk's map. This is the best lead we have. The stature of people hundreds of years ago was generally smaller, so this makes sense. Besides, there has been a rockslide, which I think closed off part of the passage. It might have been wider at one time."

When Zach started back toward the other side, Hawke asked, "You don't think there is any way Maggie would come down here?"

"You saw her. She was in a cave-in with her father when she was thirteen. He died, and she was trapped until the rescuers managed to dig her out."

"That explains a lot."

"Yeah. I couldn't ask her to do that, even if she wanted to try again."

Hawke sent him a sharp look. "Even if that meant the bad guys got the codices?"

"Yes."

"Whoa, cousin. You've got it bad."

Zach emerged from the pool. "Got what bad?"

"Surely you know what being in love feels like. You were in love with your wife. Have you already forgotten?"

"I'm not in love," Zach immediately said, then realized he shouldn't have spoken in haste. Was he in love with Maggie? They hadn't known each other long. Then he remembered he hadn't known his wife for long when he'd first realized he was in love with her. "You of all people shouldn't speak of being in love," Zach said.

"Just because I've sworn off women doesn't mean you have to," Hawke said.

A noise pierced the cavern. Zach whirled toward the sound while Hawke drew his gun. A light shone in the dark shadows.

"It's me, Maggie."

"Maggie!" How much had she heard? Zach wondered, and hurried toward her. "Is something wrong?"

"It's him. I mean, Joe Bailey. He's here with two other men."

Hawke approached. "How? He should be in federal custody by now."

She shook her head. "I didn't stay to ask him. They may be about half an hour behind me if they followed the same path."

"I don't understand how they solved the code so quickly. They haven't had the diary and map for long." Zach looked over Maggie's shoulder toward the direction she had come from.

Worry creased Zach's face, and she wanted to smooth the lines away, but there wasn't any time. "What should we do?"

"You say there are three of them?" Hawke checked his gun.

"Yes. Armed and mean looking."

"We'll have to surprise them." Zach scanned the cavern. "There aren't many places to hide here, but there are places back in the last chamber."

"Then let's go." Maggie started to swing around when Zach stopped her.

"No. We only have two guns. I'm not putting you in danger with nothing to protect yourself."

Maggie did her own inspection of the cavern. "Where do you want me to hide? Under the water?"

Zach's eyes lit up. "I think we found the place where the codices are, or at least how to get to them, but we can't fit through the slot in the wall. You should be able to. You can hide in there until it's safe to come out."

"Where?" Maggie didn't want to be alone anymore. She'd pushed herself to get this far because she'd had to warn Zach and Hawke.

Zach slipped out of his backpack and plopped the bag on the floor. "I'll show you. Where's the gun?"

Maggie delved into her bag and produced the weapon. Zach passed it to Hawke, then took her hand and led her into the pool. Cold water seeped into her boots. As she went deeper into it, she shook. Before long it was up to her chest, and she held her backpack above her head to keep it dry.

Zach halted in front of the far wall where a rockslide had occurred. How recently, she couldn't tell. The realization that it had sometime in the past, cutting off access to the rest of the cave, frightened her—especially since the mountain was still rumbling.

"You want me to go through that?" She pointed a shaky finger at the small opening.

"You're the only one who can. Hawke and I are too big, as you can see."

"I—I—can't…" She clamped her mouth closed. She was the only one who could complete the job unless they left and came back with someone else. She didn't want that. This had been Gramps's dream, to find the Aztec codices. She would do it for him, for Zach. "I'll do it."

He clasped her upper arms and hauled her to him, then planted a quick kiss on her mouth before releasing her. "None of the men with Bailey are small, are they?"

"No. About the same size as he is."

"Then you'll be safe in there, and Hawke and I can be free to do what we have to." As she neared the slot, he took her bag. "I'll hand it to you so you can pull it through behind you."

Maggie squeezed into the opening sideways, the rough surface of the stones scraping across her body. She took her backpack and dragged it in after her. Her pulse rate increased the farther away from Zach she went, but she saw ahead that the narrow passage ended.

Lord, watch over Zach and Hawke. Don't let anything happen to them.

She slipped from the slot and entered a chamber, so large the lamp on her helmet—which she had recovered, thankfully—didn't shine on the far walls. After switching her lamp to the brightest setting, she walked a few paces forward, directing the beam in a sweep in front of her. Breathtaking formations littered the floor of the cavern, glistening white, some delicate like the petals of flowers.

Awed by God's artistry, she basked in the beauty about her, turning in a slow circle to inspect the room. For that brief moment she forgot that she was alone in a dark chamber, hundreds of feet below the earth, trapped. Then something along the wall to the left of her caught her attention. It glinted. She stepped closer and bent down, brushing the dust and dirt from its surface. A cup. She lifted it up to inspect it better.

It was a jewel-encrusted vessel of gold.

"Let's rock and roll. We've got some people to take care of." Zach checked his gun and grabbed his extra clip.

"We need to make sure they are all through the bolt-hole before we do anything. We wouldn't want one getting away." Hawke put his backpack next to Zach's on the floor near the entrance into the pool chamber, and grabbed some rope.

"We'd better hurry. We have to assume they have the map and have figured out that it's a diagram of this cave. It won't take them long to find this." Zach moved toward the short passage that led to the next cavern and went first.

In the cavern he and Hawke found places to conceal themselves behind two hoodoos standing sentry near the bolt-hole. While they waited for Bailey and his two men, Zach's thoughts went to Maggie. Was she all right? He knew the extent of her fear, but she'd come after him and Hawke anyway. The realization of what she had done to warn them astounded him. Other than Kate rescuing him in the Amazon, he had never had someone do that for him.

He was almost afraid to examine his feelings about Maggie. He'd loved Helen so much and had given up part of what he loved to do for her. Could he be happy doing it again?

The sound of someone coming through the bolt-hole pushed the unanswered question to the back of his mind. When they got out of the cave alive, he would have to deal with his personal life. But first he had to take care of the men after them.

Zach signaled to Hawke that he was ready. Bailey slid through the opening and immediately straightened, alert. His lamp swept a wide arc around the chamber as the next man came through. The last one followed a minute later. When all three had finished their visual inspections, they started forward.

They would have to walk between the two hoodoos to get to the passage that led to the next chamber, the only passage from this cavern. Bailey saw his target and went first. As he passed, Zach moved around to continue to hide until all three were through the narrow passageway between the two stone sentries.

Zach stepped into the path with Hawke right behind him and leveled his gun at the three men. "That's as far as you go."

All of them whirled, fumbling to get their weapons.

"I wouldn't try anything if I were you." Zach pointed his revolver at Bailey, the leader.

"Drop your guns slowly, then your backpacks." Hawke came forward. "It's nice to see you again, Bailey. How kind of you to turn yourself in, although it would have been more convenient to do it at the station."

Bailey growled his anger, his eyes full of fury. "I have a knack for escaping."

"Not this time." Zach smiled. The sight of the rope hanging off Bailey's bag brought back memories of when Maggie had tied him up at her grandfather's house. Now he found humor in the situation. "Take that rope and bind your friends' feet and hands."

Bailey grumbled something under his breath but complied, moving to the smaller of the two men and twisting the length around his feet first.

"Pull it tighter. Don't think I won't inspect your work." Zach kept his attention on Bailey, but said to Hawke, "It's such a shame that people nowadays just don't take pride in their workmanship like they used to."

"Personally, I don't understand how Bailey would work for someone who killed his partner. There's no honor among thieves," Hawke replied.

"Or friendship obviously," Zach saw Bailey stiffen.

When Bailey stood, his two cohorts tied up on the floor of the cavern, he balled his hands at his side. Angry darts shot from his eyes.

"Now it's your turn," Zach said. "Get down between your two partners." Zach gave Hawke his gun and took the rope his cousin had brought with him, then he cautiously approached Bailey. After securing the large man, he checked the other two. He tightened the length around the smaller one's hands, then scooped up their guns, which he passed to Hawke to put in his backpack.

"A word of advice—you might want to find someone else to partner with. Bailey's partners turn up dead." Zach backed away from the trio, satisfied they weren't going anywhere anytime soon. "Care to share who you are working for?"

Bailey glared at him. "We won't double-cross the man who hired us."

"Aah, so you do know who paid you." Hawke returned Zach's gun to him. "Too bad you aren't talking. It could have helped your case." He turned to the other men. "Either one of you want to cut a deal?"

Both men looked toward Bailey, who cackled. "I ain't no fool. They don't know."

"Oh, well, I thought I would give you a last chance." Hawke started for the passage into the pool chamber.

One of the men shouted, "You can't leave us here!"

Zach twisted around and grinned. "Sure we can. We ain't no fools, either. There is no safe way we could escort you out of this cave."

As he disappeared into the passage, he heard Bailey telling the man to shut up and stop moaning.

"A job well done if I say so myself," Zach said with a chuckle.

"When we get out of here, I can radio for help to transport them out," Hawke said.

"Perhaps by that time, Bailey will have rethought his stance on making a deal."

"Don't count on it, Zach. I've seen his kind before. Whoever he's working for isn't a nice man to cross."

A chill went through Zach. They were definitely crossing this mysterious man.

Out of a sarcophagus filled with Aztec artifacts, Maggie lifted one of the codices. It was a book written on deerskin. It had been preserved by the stone coffin. Although there were abundant treasures before her, this was what had started it all. According to her grandfather, because of the Spanish purge when they conquered the Aztecs, no books had survived, even though they had been common among the Aztecs.

She emptied her bag, then carefully laid the three codices in it. She hated leaving all the other artifacts, but someone else would have to come back for them. Looking around at the darkness that hemmed her in, she shivered. A panicky feeling crept up her spine.

No bones had been in the stonelike coffin, but its shape unnerved her. She needed to get out of there. She rose with her backpack in hand and started for the narrow passage.

Another rumble beneath her feet froze her. The sound of rocks hitting the floor thundered through her mind.

THIRTEEN

The crash of rocks falling echoed through the chamber. The sound came from the hidden cavern. Zach thrust the gun into Hawke's hand and hurried toward the pool. "I've got to get Maggie out of there."

As he tore across the water, stirring up the silt, all he could think about was Maggie trapped by tons of rocks, as she had been before with her father. He'd done this to her. He shouldn't have insisted she hide in the other chamber. The codices weren't worth it. Nothing was.

Father, please keep her safe.

At the slit in the rocks, he pressed his face against their rough surface and shouted, "Maggie! Maggie, are you okay?" His pulse raced.

One heartbeat. Two. Silence.

"Maggie!"

"I'm coming." She coughed. "Some rocks slid down on the other side of the cavern. The dust is thick in here."

Another cough filled his ears like sweet music. She was alive. *Thank you, Father.*

He stepped back, seeing her light through the haze of dust coming toward him. When she appeared, he assisted her through the passage, then pulled her against him, his arms tight about her. He didn't want to let her go.

She chuckled and mumbled against his chest, "I've got to breathe, Zach."

"Sorry." He pulled back and ran his gaze over her beautiful features, saw the dirt smudges on her face. He wiped his finger across them. "What have you been doing? Playing in the dirt?"

Smiling, she leaned back. "Something like that. I've got the codices. They're in my backpack. Three of them." She opened her bag to show him the codices.

"Three? I'd have been happy for one or two, but three! Are they readable, intact?" Excited, Zach slipped one of them out of her backpack.

"Yes, as you can see." She took the deerskin book and secured it in her bag. "Right now I need to leave. I don't want to stay another minute in this cave."

He cupped her face, his eyes a soft gray. "We caught Bailey and his men. They're in the next cavern, tied up."

"Good. Let's go."

Zach waded across the pool with Maggie next to him, his arm about her shoulder. "We'll hike out and send someone else for the three men."

"Will they be okay until then?"

Zach peered down at her upturned face. "They are in God's hands. It's too dangerous for us to escort them out. I didn't see any evidence of any recent rockslides in that chamber, so hopefully they'll be okay until we get some help."

"I'll pray for them and us. I don't want any more deaths associated with these codices."

As they approached Hawke at the edge of the water, Zach said, "I agree. Praying will help." *We'll need it,* he thought silently, remembering the long climb to the entrance.

When Maggie emerged from the dark cave, blackness surrounded her. She looked up at the star-studded sky and chuckled. "How appropriate. Nighttime. All I've been thinking about was getting out into the sunlight."

Hawke came out of the entrance. "When you're in a cave, you have no sense of time."

Exhausted, she collapsed on the ground near where the tent equipment lay. She fingered the canvas. "All I want to do is curl up and go to sleep."

"Not a bad idea." Zach picked up the tent.

"While you set up camp, I'll hike down to my Jeep and call for help. As much as I would like to leave the trio down in the cave, we'll need to stay here until help arrives, especially since Maggie told us they slashed our tires, and we forgot to search them for their car keys." Hawke, with a flashlight, started down the mountain.

Although she hurt all over from using muscles she'd forgotten she had, Maggie began to push herself to her feet.

Zach stopped her. "Stay put. I'll take care of making camp. You rest."

"You've got to be as tired as I am."

He shook his head as he slipped out of his backpack

and put his gun away. After placing the bag by a huge boulder, he stretched the canvas out on the ground near Maggie. "I didn't face a fear today. You did."

"Only because the Lord was with me every step of the way," she said, then silently added, *and I couldn't let the man I love die.*

He pushed a stake into the ground. "With Him by our sides we can do some amazing things."

Maggie closed her eyes and listened to Zach finish putting up the tent then gather some sticks for a fire. Knowing he was nearby lulled her to sleep.

"Look who we have here," a man said in accented English.

Maggie's eyes flew open at the sound of the familiar voice. Darkness greeted her. For a moment she didn't know where she was. She reached out and grazed her fingertips along the canvas of the tent. Somehow Zach must have carried her inside when she fell asleep. Through a narrow slit by the tent's door she saw a fire, and Zach's angry face. She clambered to a sitting position and inched closer to the opening.

"Where are my men?" Señor Santos came into Maggie's view.

Zach shrugged. "What men?"

"I know they are here. They contacted me before going into the cave."

Behind Señor Santos stood another man she could only describe as a hulking bodyguard, with a .44 Magnum in his hand. The Hulk gestured with his gun for Hawke to join Zach by the fire. The Mexican businessman didn't seem to carry a gun, so if Maggie could take care of the bodyguard…

She fumbled around in the tent for some kind of weapon. There wasn't anything, but then she remembered that Zach had placed his backpack with his gun in it along the boulder behind where he had set up the tent. If she could just get it, then she might be able to turn the tables on Señor Santos.

She scrambled to the back of the tent and tugged the canvas up, then crawled under it. The bag was a few feet away, with one of those feet exposing her to anyone who was looking toward the tent.

Lord, be with me.

She started to sneak low toward the boulder when she heard Señor Santos ask, "Where is Dr. Somers? In there?"

Maggie stopped. The sounds of movement in front of the tent, then the flap being wrenched open caused sweat to coat her.

"As you can see, she isn't with us. Why would I share this discovery with her? All I wanted from her was the diary. A Collier doesn't work with a Somers."

Although she knew the ruthless words Zach said were a lie to protect her, they chilled her.

"Forget my men. What I want to know is, where are the codices?"

Judging by the sound of Santos's voice, he must have moved back toward the fire. Maggie again started for the backpack and managed to snag a strap. Slowly she tugged it toward her, determined not to make any noise. When the bag was hidden by the tent, she snatched it up and carefully unzipped it. Delving inside, she felt around for the gun, praying it was still in the backpack where she'd seen Zach put it.

"They're in the cave. If this is even the right place."

Zach's words reminded her of the urgency of the situation. Señor Santos wasn't a man who would take no for an answer. Finally she grasped the metal of the barrel. When she brought the gun out, she checked the clip then took off the safety.

"I am not a patient man, Dr. Collier. These codiçes are part of my heritage. They do not belong to you and I will do anything to keep them out of your hands. *Anything*. I don't need but one of you, so your cousin is expendable. Xavier, take care of him."

"Wait!"

Zach's shout bombarded off the rocks and propelled Maggie into action. She would only have one chance. *Please, Lord, help me to remember Gramps's lessons.*

She readied the gun, leaped to her feet and took aim at the bodyguard as he raised his .44 toward Hawke. She squeezed off a shot while everyone's attention turned to her. The bullet ricocheted off the rock near the bodyguard, missing her target by inches.

But the distraction was enough that Hawke launched himself toward the bodyguard, coming in low while Zach came in high. The man fell to the ground. Santos made a move toward the three wrestling men.

Maggie stepped out from behind the tent. "Stay where you are."

The Mexican businessman turned toward her, glaring. Then a smile slithered across his face. "I do not think you will shoot me." He started for her.

She leveled the gun at him and pulled the trigger. The bullet hit the dirt at his feet.

Santos laughed. "See? You do not have what it takes to be a killer. But I do." He took another step toward her.

"That was a warning shot," she said in the toughest voice she could muster. Sweat rolled down her face. She willed her hand to be steady as she lifted the gun toward his torso.

"*Doctor* Somers, I have nothing to lose and everything to gain." Santos came another step closer.

"But I have no qualms about pulling this trigger." Zach cocked his gun, the barrel pressed into the back of Santos's head.

Maggie glanced behind the pair and saw Hawke tying up the unconscious bodyguard. Dropping her arm with the gun to her side, she nearly collapsed. By sheer willpower she held herself up and walked to Hawke to give him the weapon.

Then she sank to the ground.

Hours later Maggie sat on a boulder at the bottom of the mountain where the cave was, cradling a cup of coffee as the sun rose, streaking the eastern horizon with fingers of rose, orange and pinks in the midst of the clear blue sky. It would be a beautiful day, and for the first time in over a week, she could look forward to that.

She had her life back.

Or did she?

She had been raised to hate anyone with the last

name Collier. But she didn't hate Zach. She loved him. *What am I going to do about it?* She didn't have an answer to that question. She was too tired and mentally exhausted.

Zach approached her. "Ready to go?"

"I was hours ago." She scanned the people who swarmed the area. Federal agents had arrived an hour ago and had taken over, hustling Señor Santos and his bodyguard away. Shortly after that, rescuers had come and were now going into the cave to bring out the three men tied up in the cavern.

"I don't know about you, but I could sleep for the next several days." Zach helped her down from the boulder. "We'll be sorting all of this out for a while."

"Will it interfere with you going on the expedition in a few weeks?" She would need to get used to not having him around 24/7. He would be leaving for the jungle soon, and her life practicing medicine in Santa Fe would resume. The thought of them going their separate ways saddened her.

"No, but the lack of Santos's money will."

"I'm so sorry. Will you have enough money to fund it completely?"

He opened the passenger door for her. "Mr. Wright might increase his donation, so maybe."

Maggie slipped into the SUV, which had new tires on it now, and watched as Zach said a few words to Hawke. Then Zach rounded the car and climbed inside. "Is he leaving, too?" she asked, indicating Hawke.

"Soon. He told me the FBI wants to talk with all of us tomorrow at his police station. I told him we would be there." He started the engine. "Evelyn wants us to stay with her so we won't have so far to travel."

"Personally, that sounds wonderful. I want to thank her for all she's done. This will give me the opportunity."

He backed away from the mountain and followed the dirt road toward the highway. "You know we need to talk."

"I know, but I'm so exhausted I don't know how much sense I would make."

"Sleep. I'll wake you at Evelyn's."

Maggie snuggled against the door. Zach knew the instant she fell asleep. Her face relaxed, all anxiety gone from her. He slowed to turn onto the highway, and studied her features for a few seconds.

What am I going to do?

He didn't have an answer. He loved her, but was it enough? Their life goals were different. They hadn't known each other for long. Could he put his heart on the line again and risk getting hurt? His marriage to Helen had been great, but the pain of her death had nearly crippled him emotionally.

And worse yet, he couldn't shake the nagging feeling that this wasn't over with. Yes, Santos was behind hiring Bailey and Huffman. But how did Santos know about the map and the diary? Who had told him?

"This was delicious, Evelyn. Thanks for fixing us dinner." Maggie rose to clear the dishes from the kitchen table.

"That's the least I could do for you all after you spent

most of the day down at the station being interviewed." Evelyn came to her feet. "Sit. You're a guest in my house."

Zach's cousin's voice brooked no argument. Maggie took her seat between Hawke and Zach. "At least that's behind us and the codices are in safe hands."

Zach leaned back in his chair. "And I think they will end up in the museum at the college eventually. A tribute to our grandfathers."

"They would like that." Evelyn stacked the dishes by the sink. "They started out as a team, and they are ending as one. You two have mended the rift between the families."

"I've volunteered to help bring out the rest of the treasure." Hawke went to the stove and poured himself some decaf coffee. "I know you won't have time, Zach, with your upcoming expedition."

"Yeah, thankfully that is back on. I was worried, with the arrest of Santos, but Mr. Wright agreed to increase his donation. The next few weeks will be hectic."

Hawke laughed. "You think? Let's see, you've got the end of the semester, the completion of the plans for your trip. Yeah, I would say you're gonna be busy." He waggled his eyebrows at Maggie. "Care to join me and represent the Somers in recovering the treasure?"

The idea of going back into the cave drove terror into her heart. "No! My adventure has come to an end. I have a dull life of treating patients waiting for me in Santa Fe." She placed an elbow on the table and cradled her chin. "You know that cavern where the treasure is kept is unstable. There was evidence of several rockslides. Please be careful, especially since you will have to dig your way into it."

"Yeah, not too many people are your size, and from your description of what is there, it would be difficult to get all the artifacts out without widening the opening." Zach sipped his coffee.

"Enough people have lost their lives over the treasure." Maggie wondered how many others besides the ones in modern times.

"But to think a sect of Aztecs spirited part of their heritage away right under the Spanish conquerors' noses." Evelyn said as she came back to the table.

"Only because Father Santiago helped them," Maggie said, wishing Gramps were here to be in the middle of this discussion. For that matter, she wished Zach's grandfather were here, too, basking in the knowledge that the codices really existed and had finally been discovered.

"It's interesting that he didn't go along with the plan to destroy all traces of the Aztec culture. Most unusual, especially for a monk." Hawke scooted his chair back and stood, stretching.

Zach finished his drink. "He was an unusual man. He wanted the Indians to retain their culture but embrace Christ. I wonder how successful he was with the Aztecs he traveled with. His journal never said anything beyond that he had converted the leader to Christianity."

"I like to think once the leader became a Christian the others followed." Hawke pushed his chair against the table.

Maggie looked at each person in the kitchen. "There are still some unanswered questions."

"Like who betrayed one of our grandfathers and told Señor Santos about the diary and map?" Zach took his cup over to the sink and rinsed it out.

"And how did they know your every move?" Hawke crossed the room to the back door.

"We may never know the answers to those questions. Señor Santos isn't talking, and I don't think the others know." Zach rubbed the nape of his neck. "That's what I'm worried about. That person is still out there."

Hawke opened the door. "I've got to feed the animals. Are you two heading home tonight?"

Maggie answered, "Yes," a second before Zach did.

"Then drive safely back to town. I'll keep you informed of any progress in the case. Who knows? Maybe Señor Santos will change his mind, confess all and tell us everything we need to know."

Zach's laugh held no humor as his cousin left. "Thanks again, Evelyn, for everything. We'd better leave." He embraced her, kissing her cheek.

"Don't be a stranger. Come see me before you leave for the jungle." Evelyn shifted toward Maggie. "And the same goes for you. Don't be a stranger. I hope you'll come see me from time to time."

Maggie rose and gave the older Indian woman a hug. "After what we went through together, there's no way I wouldn't. How's next weekend?" she asked with a laugh.

"Tomorrow's fine by me. With you two around, there's never a dull moment."

Five minutes later, with the SUV packed, they were in the car and heading toward the highway that led to Albuquerque. Evelyn's last words played in Maggie's mind over and over: *never a dull moment*. She got the feeling that where Zach went excitement followed. But that wasn't her way of life. Tomorrow she needed to get back to her routine and paticnts. The real world awaited her.

Zach pulled into Maggie's driveway and switched off the engine. It seemed like a lifetime had passed since Maggie had seen her house. She stared at it as if she hadn't seen it before.

"I guess I'd better go in," she said reluctantly, a sadness enveloping her.

"After what happened last time, I'd like to check out the house, if that's okay."

The reminder of the incident that had occurred a week before made her hesitate.

"Maggie?"

"Yes. Yes, that's fine." She thrust open the door and climbed from the SUV.

Zach carried her overnight bag while she rummaged in her large purse until she found her key, and unlocked her house. Inside she was again struck by the havoc. All around her was evidence of the destruction that Joe Bailey had caused in her home.

"I'd forgotten all about this," she whispered as she rotated in a slow circle in the middle of her living room.

"I'll stay and help you clean up," Zach offered.

She spun around to face him. "No! You've done

enough. I'll take care of this." She wasn't even sure why her voice sounded so forceful. Maybe if they made a clean break and went their separate ways, her heart wouldn't hurt as much. "I mean, I'm tired, and all I want to do is go to bed. You still need to drive back to Albuquerque. You told Ray you were going to be handling your classes tomorrow, and I told Carol I would be at work first thing in the morning."

He gave her a strange look, his forehead creased. "Okay, if that's the way you want it."

No. Yes. She didn't know what she wanted. That was the problem. She loved him, but there were so many things that stood in their way. His work and life-style. Her past relationship. Besides, the past week had been unreal. How could a lasting love come out of that? She just needed to get back to her routine. The hurt would fade, as it had with Brad Wentworth.

"I'll check the house, then go." He walked from the living room, leaving her alone with her thoughts.

Who was she kidding? The hurt she'd suffered over Brad's betrayal had been nothing like this. She moved to the picture window that looked out over the front yard, and stared at the curtain of darkness. She wished she were better at relationships, then maybe she would know what to do.

But right now her mind was so muddled with exhaustion. Sleep was all she could handle.

"Everything looks okay." She heard him cross the living room toward the door. "Good night, Maggie."

Something in his voice pulled at her heart. She slid a glance toward him and caught a glimpse of his strong profile set in a neutral expression as he disappeared into the foyer.

"Goodbye, Zach," she whispered in a raw voice, not sure if he even heard her. But emotions swelled, closing her throat. Tears misted her eyes.

At the sound of the front door shutting, one tear rolled down her cheek. She brushed it away. She would not cry. Their adventure was over, and she needed to get on with her life—without him.

Zach climbed into the rented SUV and pulled out of Maggie's driveway. His teeth clenched in frustration. Her goodbye had sounded so final. Yes, there were obstacles in the way of having a meaningful relationship with Maggie, and maybe this was for the best. How could he ask her to give up her practice to come with him on his expeditions? What kind of marriage would it be if he was gone a lot doing fieldwork? In the cave he had encountered microorganisms that he wanted to study after his trip to the jungle. He got excited just thinking about all the possibilities available in caves around the world.

Maybe this wasn't the real thing. He needed to get back to his life and finalize the plans for the expedition. He needed to keep busy, and then perhaps he could forget the connection he felt with Maggie Somers.

The next morning bright sunlight streamed through the kitchen windows. A cup of coffee in hand, Maggie lugged her large purse to the table and sat. She was an organized person, and it was time to clean out her bag, get her life in order again. Her purse weighed a ton, and over the past week with Zach all she had done was stuff things into it, even gum wrappers and sales receipts.

She dumped the contents out. A lipstick rolled off the table and plunked onto the tile floor. Some coins she hadn't had time to put in her wallet scattered over the wooden surface of the table. Crumpled-up tissues and a smashed candy bar caught her attention.

Although she had managed to sleep some the night before, a lump was ever present in her throat, making a mockery of her declaration that she would get her life back on track—minus Zach Collier.

Remembering the couple of times she and Zach had eaten a candy bar this past week, she touched the bar and considered unwrapping it for all of two seconds. Then she thought of what she usually had for breakfast—a bowl of cereal with fruit. No, she would find something other than candy to eat. She tossed the bar into the trash, then turned her attention to the other items on the table, picking up her wallet to put it back into her bag.

Next to her checkbook was a small black object that looked like a flash drive for a computer. She'd never seen it before. Had Zach put one with the diary on it in her purse? Why didn't he tell her if he had?

She walked into her office in the second bedroom, stepping around the mess still littering her house from the break-in, and booted up her laptop. She stuck the flash drive into the USB port and waited for something to come up on the screen. Nothing appeared. Strange.

Picking up the phone on the desk, she punched in Zach's home number. When he answered, a thrill at the sound of his deep baritone voice momentarily distracted her.

"Maggie, is something wrong?"

"Maybe," she answered, needing to sit in the chair, her legs suddenly weak.

"What?"

The urgency in his one word caused her to quickly say, "The flash drive of the diary you put in my purse doesn't work."

"I didn't give you a flash drive. I haven't had a chance to copy it yet, and besides, I was hoping the police would recover the real journal from Santos."

"You didn't?" She pulled the black object out of her laptop and examined it. "Then what is this?"

"I can be there in an hour. My first class isn't until one. Will you be at work?"

"Yes, but—"

"See you in an hour then."

He hung up before she could tell him it wasn't necessary to come all the way to Santa Fe. A part of her wasn't ready to see him so soon. But then there was a part that was wondering if she should change into something more feminine than tailored black slacks and a long-sleeved white shirt.

Zach stared at the phone he had put back in its cradle. He couldn't believe he had said that to Maggie. Why was he torturing himself by insisting he come see her? All that was going to do was prolong the pain. Hadn't he settled this with himself last night?

No. That was just it. He hadn't slept at all, even though he had been so tired he hadn't thought he could keep his eyes open. He'd proven himself wrong. He'd lain in bed, staring up at the ceiling. By the early hours of the morning, he knew he didn't want to end what they had started. He loved her and wanted to see if there was a way they could work it out.

When the phone rang again, he jumped, not expecting another call so early. Would it be Maggie, telling him not to come? He almost didn't pick up the receiver until he spotted his caller ID and saw that the number was the rehabilitation center where his grandfather had spent his last days.

"Dr. Collier, this is Cassie. I know we talked a few days ago, and I told you no one remembered anyone else. Well, I was wrong. I saw Fred this morning in the break room reading the newspaper when I took my lunch in to put it in the refrigerator. He commented on the picture on the front page, of Señor Santos. When he saw the photo, he remembered seeing him at the center with Dr. Kingston on the day your grandfather died. I thought I should tell you since the write-up said Señor Santos had been accused of trying to kill you."

As Zach listened to Cassie talk, his grip on the receiver tightened until his knuckles were white. John Kingston? One of Granddad's protégés? Was it just a coincidence they'd been together, or had John brought Santos to the center for a sinister purpose? Why would

Santos be at the center seeing his grandfather unless he was after information?

"Dr. Collier? Are you there?"

"Sorry, Cassie. I was just thinking about what you said. I really appreciate your calling. This might be important. Thanks."

He replaced the phone in its cradle, snatched up his keys and headed for his car. He would see Maggie, then pay John a visit. If the museum curator and supposed friend had betrayed Red, John would regret ever having done it.

Maggie rose when Zach entered her office, then wished she hadn't. The sight of Zach so close turned her legs to jelly. She lowered herself onto her chair, clasping its arms. It was too soon. She wasn't ready to see him.

He crossed the room, hesitated for a few seconds then took the seat in front of her desk, as though they were doctor and patient. "What did you find?"

She palmed the black object, bent forward and slid it toward him. "I thought of opening it up, but I didn't want to do anything until you checked it out. I thought maybe you had forgotten—"

"I didn't forget putting this in your purse." His jaw hardened. "I've never seen this before." He withdrew a pocketknife and pried the casing open. He lifted a microchip out of it. "I'm thinking this is a tracking device, and this is how Bailey and Huffman knew where we were."

"Okay, then how did it get into my purse?"

"Good question." He set the black object on the desk. "I got a call from Cassie. One of the orderlies who worked in Granddad's unit remembered seeing Santos with John Kingston at the center the day my grandfather died."

"So you think that John betrayed your grandfather?"

Zach nodded, the hard lines of his face sharpening even more.

"There would be no reason Santos would visit your grandfather with John?"

"None that I can think of, but I'll give the man a chance to explain."

A memory, just out of focus, niggled her mind. "I'm missing something. This reminds me of when I was trying to remember the maps Dad used to draw of the caves." She looked toward the door. "I want to come with you."

"I thought you had patients today."

"Not until this afternoon. I had a lot of paperwork to catch up on, but maybe I'll think of it as we drive to the museum. Or seeing John will jog my memory."

Zach shot to his feet. "Okay, then let's go."

Maggie remembered touring the museum less than a week ago with Santos as her guide. The man behind all the murders had been so polite and gentlemanly, so close to her that evening he could have strangled her. She shuddered.

How did a person really know anyone? Again her opinion of someone had been totally wrong. Doubts beset her as she walked toward John's office at the back of the museum.

The man's secretary welcomed Zach with a huge smile. "I read about your latest adventure in the paper this morning. My, you live quite an exciting life."

Zach winced. "Exciting isn't all it's cracked up to be. Is John in?"

"For you, anytime."

Zach crossed to the door while the secretary informed her employer he had visitors. Maggie wondered just how thrilled the curator would be when he heard why they were there.

With a smile on his face, John came around his desk. "This is unexpected. Are the authorities going to release the items in the cave sooner than you thought when you called yesterday?"

Zach kept a few feet between him and John. "No, I came about something else. Why did you betray my grandfather?"

John blinked, then stiffened, a scowl marring his features. "Betrayed...Red? I—I—would never..." His words came to a splattering halt.

"I discovered this morning that you took Santos to see my grandfather the last day he was alive. There was no reason for Santos to visit him." The hardened edge to Zach's voice knifed through the silence.

"How could you think that?" The older man's face reddened. "Your grandfather and I were good friends." John's gaze slid away, then returned to meet Zach's.

"Forgive me if I don't believe you." Sarcasm dripped off Zach's words. "Why did you do it? For money?"

The curator opened his mouth then snapped it closed, his eyes pinpoints as they drilled into Zach.

"How did you know Santos? Are you dealing in the black market? What else from the museum have you mishandled? I wonder what would happen if the records were audited."

John marched to his door and wrenched it open. "Get out. You don't have a shred of proof, or the police would be here instead of you."

"That's where Maggie and I are going next. I think they'll be interested in my little theory. It has to be for money. How much was my grandfather worth to you?"

"Get out, or I'll call the campus security to come and remove you." The curator's voice rose several levels.

Zach grabbed Maggie's hand and headed toward the entrance into the office. When he passed John, Zach paused and stabbed him with a lancing gaze.

Suddenly Maggie recalled what had been bothering her earlier. John had bumped into her in the science building when Zach and she were leaving to go to Evelyn's the day they had come for the copy of the map. John had helped her pick up her purse and put the contents back in it. He'd had the opportunity to plant the tracking device in it—he was the only one she could think of who had handled her bag. When they were outside the museum, she told Zach what she finally remembered. "Did you see him look away when he said he was a good friend of your grandfather's?" she added.

"No, I was too angry." Fury etched harsh lines into Zach's features.

"He was lying, but I don't know if we have enough for the police."

The anger siphoned from his expression, to be

replaced with a hard mask of determination. "I know. But I think I know how we can rattle his cage. Let's go. I want to visit the college president and persuade him to ask for an audit."

"Why would he do it?"

"If he wants the Aztec codices in the museum, he'll have to agree."

If sheer resolve had any impact on the records being audited, they would be by the end of that day. Maggie marveled at the force behind Zach, but then she thought about how wrong they both had been about the people involved.

Maggie looked around her living room, the last area she had put back in order after the break-in. Although there wasn't any more chaos in her house, she felt her life was a big mess. It had been five days since she had seen Zach and gone with him to the president of the college to pressure him into doing an in-depth audit of the museum's finances and its contents. Five days of trying to keep herself so busy she didn't miss him. Five days of pushing thoughts of Zach out of her mind, only to have them immediately return to plague her.

Her house, even Gramps's, was back the way it had been. She was seeing her patients, worked full days with no breaks except a few minutes at lunch to grab something to eat. She fell into bed at night totally exhausted, but she couldn't sleep.

She couldn't sever the connection she'd experienced with Zach. He dominated her every waking moment— and even what little sleep she managed. She had it bad.

And what are you going to do about it? See Zach?
Yes.
No.

The conflicting emotions swamped her. She buried her face in her hands.

Lord, what do I do? I love him. I can't fight it anymore. I know we haven't known each other long, but I feel needed, safe with him.

The sound of the doorbell jerked her up and around toward the foyer. She'd had her fill of visitors wanting to know all about her little adventure. She was tired of telling the story. Maybe if she ignored whoever was on her porch, the person would leave.

The bell rang again.

Go. Open the door.

She couldn't ignore the strong urge that propelled her forward. She placed her hand on the knob, then remembered to check the peephole. When she saw Zach, she quickly turned the handle.

He filled her entry with his commanding presence. Her gaze trekked up his long length to rest on his face, lit with a big smile and eyes only for her. She went into his embrace and instantly felt she had come home.

"May I come in?" Zach finally asked.

She leaned back, peering up at him. She wanted to run her fingers through his hair, to kiss his mouth, to continue holding him. But they needed to talk, to figure out what to do, how to make a relationship work between them.

He settled his arm along her shoulders and walked into the living room. "I'm glad you got everything taken care of here."

"I finished about half an hour ago."

"I guess I came at the right time then." He lifted one corner of his mouth as his gaze snared hers. Shifting to stand in front of her, he framed her face between his large hands. "We need to talk. I can't keep ignoring how I feel about you."

"You can't," she squeaked out in a breathless rush. The warm feel of his palms against her cheeks cemented her resolve. She wanted so much more, and until she had seen him, she hadn't realized just how much. She wanted him in her life—somehow.

"This may sound crazy, but I've fallen in love with you. I know we haven't known each other for long, but I love you, Maggie, and I want us to be together."

His declaration wiped a response from her brain. All she could do was stare at him with what she hoped was love in her gaze.

"Say something." He ran his thumb across her lips as though that would urge her to speak.

"I—I'm—speechless."

"Is that a good thing or a bad thing?" Humor danced in his eyes.

She brought her hands up to rest on his shoulders, to give her time to compose her thoughts. "It's good. I love you, Zach. I've spent the past week trying to deny it. I can't. I do, and that isn't going to change because we spend months together getting to know each other. I've seen you in some of the worst situations and I like what I've seen. I feel like I've known you for a long time, not just a few weeks."

Tenderness pushed the humor from his eyes. "That's

the way I feel. These past five days I've forced myself to stay away. Thankfully I've had a lot to do, especially with John's arrest and the expedition."

"The police finally arrested John?"

"Yes, I came right over when I heard from the detective. They caught him trying to leave the country and have charged him with a whole list of crimes, from fraud, to conspiracy to commit murder, to being a part of a black-market ring. Bailey is finally talking, and they're working on the connection between Santos and John. There's a paper trail. There usually is when money is involved."

"And it all started with that audit you insisted on. Our grandfathers will have justice after all."

"Yes," he whispered, hauling her to him and planting a kiss on her mouth. "Finally." He walked her backward until her legs encountered the couch, then he gently pushed her down. "We need to talk about what we are going to do with the rest of our lives."

"Yes." Now that she had found him she didn't want them to be apart every summer while he did his research in some exotic place in the world.

"When I figured out that I wasn't going to forget you, I knew I had to come up with a way for our relationship to work, because, Maggie, I want us to get married. I see how happy my sister and Slader are and I want that again. They didn't know each other for long, either, and they only have eyes for each other."

She wanted that, too, and if that meant she didn't see him three months out of twelve, then so be it. She would make the nine months last as if they were twelve.

"When you return from the Amazon, we can work through it."

He took her hands and held them in his lap. "No, I want you to go with me. I know I'm asking you to give up your practice for three months, but you can still be a doctor. The people I encounter on my expedition always need medical care. Often they have never seen a doctor, or only a few times in their life. You could reach so many people in need this way. Would you consider doing something like that? We would live here for nine months while I teach at the college. Then, in the summer, I can do my research trips." He quirked his mouth. "I would even move to Santa Fe."

As he explained his plan, Maggie sensed a peace spread through her. This was the Lord's answer to her prayer. She wouldn't have to give up being a doctor, and in fact, could help in places where there was little medical care. Perfect. "I would have to make arrangements with my partner, but I think it can be worked out. We have been talking about adding another doctor, anyway."

He grasped her arms. "Is that a yes to my proposal?"

"You want to marry me before you leave to go to the Amazon?"

"Why not? I don't see why we should wait. I know the jungle isn't the ideal place for a honeymoon, but we'll be together."

She smiled. "That's all that's important." She threw herself into his embrace, their mouths meeting in a kiss.

EPILOGUE

Maggie gripped the railing of the steamer as it headed down the Amazon River. In the distance a wall of green indicated the shore. The warm air encased her in a sheen of perspiration, but she was so happy she didn't care that she didn't like to sweat.

"Are you glad you're going home?" Zach came up behind her and cradled her back against him, his arms enveloping her.

Watching the muddy water rush past the boat, she said, "In my usual decisive way, I have to answer yes and no. I'm looking forward to returning to Santa Fe, but only because you'll be there."

He swung her around to face him. "No regrets?"

She shook her head. "None. I have felt so alive these past three months. I have helped many people who desperately needed my help."

"Remember that little girl in the last village we visited?"

"Yes." A picture of a child no more than five or six flashed into her mind. Adorable, but suffering from a massive infection.

"You gave her a chance to live, and her mother wanted me to give you this." He retrieved from his backpack a basket, beautifully woven in colors of red, yellow and black.

A toucan on the inside bottom drew her attention. She took it and ran her fingers over the painted bird, marveling at the artistry. "This is—this—"

"I think I've rendered you speechless for the second time in your life."

She peered up at her husband, tears of happiness blurring his image. "I love you, and thank you for opening up another world to me. I feel so alive and complete."

"Sharing with you one of the things I love to do puts me in awe that the Lord brought us together," he murmured, right before he kissed her as though he had been gone for three months and had missed her every second.

Dear Reader,

This is a sequel to my January 2007 Love Inspired Suspense, *Heart of the Amazon*. I love to write books with a strong adventure element in them. They are some of my favorite books to read. I hope you enjoyed the merry ride I took Zach and Maggie on.

I also enjoyed revisiting New Mexico, a beautiful state. My family and I have spent several vacations exploring the state and all its treasures, from deserts to mountains.

I love hearing from readers. You can contact me at P.O. Box 2074, Tulsa, OK 74101, or visit my Web site at www.margaretdaley.com, where you can sign up for my quarterly newsletter.

Best wishes,

Margaret Daley

QUESTIONS FOR DISCUSSION

1. As I was writing this book, I thought of this story as a cross between the movie *National Treasure* and the Indiana Jones series. What elements of those films are reflected in *Buried Secrets?*

2. Zach's partner betrayed him. He was leery of trusting someone after that. How did his faith help him get past that betrayal?

3. Hate can fester in a person's heart and cause him or her not to live life to the fullest. That is what happened with Gramps. How should he have handled the situation between himself and Red Collier?

4. Who is your favorite character in *Buried Secrets?* Why?

5. Maggie had to learn to put her trust in the Lord to save Zach. She remembered Psalm 23 as she was making her way through the cave. Can you think of other verses that would have helped her through her ordeal?

6. After losing her grandfather, Maggie turned away from the Lord. She had a hard time understanding how He could take all her loved ones away. Has something in your life made you question the Lord's plan for you? How have you dealt with it?

7. Have you ever had to face your worst nightmare, as Maggie had to? What helped you get through it? Did you rely on your faith?

8. Which secondary character added the most to the story? Why?

9. Have you ever had to work with someone you didn't like? Maggie thought that was the case with Zach. After all, the Colliers and the Somers didn't like each other. What helped you make the situation work?

10. Family is important to both Zach and Maggie. Zach turned to his family to help him, whereas Maggie was devastated that her immediate family was all gone. How important is your family to you?

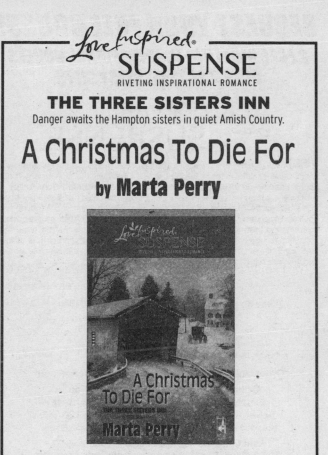

REQUEST YOUR FREE BOOKS!

2 FREE RIVETING INSPIRATIONAL NOVELS PLUS 2 FREE MYSTERY GIFTS

Love Inspired®
SUSPENSE

YES! Please send me 2 FREE Love Inspired® Suspense novels and my 2 FREE mystery gifts. After receiving them, if I don't wish to receive any more books, I can return the shipping statement marked "cancel." If I don't cancel, I will receive 4 brand-new novels every month and be billed just $3.99 per book in the U.S. or $4.74 per book in Canada, plus 25¢ shipping and handling per book and applicable taxes, if any*. That's a savings of 20% off the cover price! I understand that accepting the 2 free books and gifts places me under no obligation to buy anything. I can always return a shipment and cancel at any time. Even if I never buy another book from Steeple Hill, the two free books and gifts are mine to keep forever.

123 IDN EL5H   323 IDN ELQH

Name	(PLEASE PRINT)	
Address		Apt. #
City	State/Prov.	Zip/Postal Code

Signature (if under 18, a parent or guardian must sign)

Order online at www.LoveInspiredSuspense.com

Or mail to Steeple Hill Reader Service™:

IN U.S.A.: P.O. Box 1867, Buffalo, NY 14240-1867
IN CANADA: P.O. Box 609, Fort Erie, Ontario L2A 5X3

Not valid to current Love Inspired Suspense subscribers.

**Want to try two free books from another series?
Call 1-800-873-8635 or visit www.morefreebooks.com**

* Terms and prices subject to change without notice. NY residents add applicable sales tax. Canadian residents will be charged applicable provincial taxes and GST. This offer is limited to one order per household. All orders subject to approval. Credit or debit balances in a customer's account(s) may be offset by any other outstanding balance owed by or to the customer. Please allow 4 to 6 weeks for delivery.

Your Privacy: Steeple Hill is committed to protecting your privacy. Our Privacy Policy is available online at www.eHarlequin.com or upon request from the Reader Service. From time to time we make our lists of customers available to reputable firms who may have a product or service of interest to you. If you would prefer we not share your name and address, please check here. ☐

LISUS07

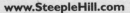

Love Inspired
SUSPENSE

TITLES AVAILABLE NEXT MONTH

Don't miss these four stories in November

A CHRISTMAS TO DIE FOR by Marta Perry
The Three Sisters Inn
Tyler Dunn came to Rachel Hampton's inn seeking justice for a decades-old crime. She wanted to trust the handsome architect, but his inquiries opened up old family secrets and turned her Christmas season amid the Plain People into a hazardous holiday.

STRANGER IN THE SHADOWS by Shirlee McCoy
After a heartbreaking tragedy, Chloe Davidson had relocated to sleepy Lakeview, Virginia, where handsome minister Ben Avery had welcomed her. Yet Chloe had an inkling that a stalker was waiting to strike. Had her place of refuge turned into a dangerous hideaway?

THE PRICE OF REDEMPTION by Pamela Tracy
There was a body in his shed, but Eric Santellis had an alibi. He'd been wrongfully imprisoned when the murder had occurred. When the body was identified as police officer Ruth Atkins's long-dead husband, Eric knew he had to help Ruth—who'd fought to see him exonerated—catch the real killer.

CRADLE OF SECRETS by Lisa Mondello
A shocking secret about her birth sent Tammie Gardner across the country on a mission to find the truth. Dylan Montgomery had reasons of his own for wanting to solve the mystery. But the answers they uncover lead to deadly consequences neither of them are prepared for.

LISCNM1007